S0-AEW-405

Her lovely eyes raised to his.

There was within those warm brown depths a gentleness that made him want to reach out and touch her. He put his hands behind his back, locking the fingers together. "Very good," he said, trying to keep his tone instructional.

"What does the woman do next?" she asked, still gazing into his eyes.

Nathaniel cleared his throat. "Once the man returns the woman's look, she looks away." She did as he instructed, lowering her eyelids until he could see nothing but the lashes that rested upon the satiny smoothness of her cheekbones.

"Is there more?" she asked.

He nodded. "You may wish to stand just that extra step closer, and when you do . . ."

"Like this?" she asked, moving to within inches of him. "Shall I touch you now?"

Nathan was not certain what he should answer. Wisdom told him he should say nay, but the man in him wanted to bid her touch him immediately. . . .

Also by Martha Kirkland

To Catch a Scoundrel

~

Martha Kirkland

A SIGNET BOOK

SIGNET
Published by the Penguin Group
Penguin Putnam Inc., 375 Hudson Street,
New York, New York 10014, U.S.A.
Penguin Books Ltd, 27 Wrights Lane,
London W8 5TZ, England
Penguin Books Australia Ltd,
Ringwood, Victoria, Australia
Penguin Books Canada Ltd, 10 Alcorn Avenue,
Toronto, Ontario, Canada M4V 3B2
Penguin Books (N.Z.) Ltd, 182–190 Wairau Road,
Auckland 10, New Zealand

Penguin Books Ltd, Registered Offices:
Harmondsworth, Middlesex, England

First published by Signet, an imprint of Dutton NAL,
a member of Penguin Putnam Inc.

First Printing, March, 1999
10 9 8 7 6 5 4 3 2 1

Copyright © Martha Cotter Kirkland, 1999
All rights reserved

 REGISTERED TRADEMARK—MARCA REGISTRADA

Printed in the United States of America

Without limiting the rights under copyright reserved above, no part of this
publication may be reproduced, stored in or introduced into a retrieval system, or
transmitted, in any form, or by any means (electronic, mechanical, photocopying,
recording, or otherwise), without the prior written permission of both the copyright
owner and the above publisher of this book.

BOOKS ARE AVAILABLE AT QUANTITY DISCOUNTS WHEN USED TO PROMOTE PRODUCTS
OR SERVICES. FOR INFORMATION PLEASE WRITE TO PREMIUM MARKETING DIVISION,
PENGUIN PUTNAM INC., 375 HUDSON STREET, NEW YORK, NY 10014.

If you purchased this book without a cover you should be aware that this book
is stolen property. It was reported as "unsold and destroyed" to the publisher
and neither the author nor the publisher has received any payment for this
"stripped book."

To my Alpha Phi sisters all over the world,
especially those from Georgia State University;
and to two special fans, Shirley Trogdon,
from North Carolina, and Brenda Beck, from Alabama.

Chapter One

"You are an idiot!" Miss Eugenia Bailey muttered, not for the first time that rainy June morning. "If all I hear of the man is true, he will most likely eat you alive." That the speaker was alone in the hackney carriage made no difference to the vehemence of her observations.

With no one to deny her claims of lunacy or declare that she was, indeed, a woman of sense, she breathed deeply, hoping a cleansing breath might bolster her sagging confidence. She regretted the act on the instant, for what she got for her troubles was a sour-smelling reminder that the straw spread over the floor of the public conveyance had not undergone an overnight replacement.

Hurriedly, she searched her reticule for a handkerchief that bore the faint scent of lemon verbena, then held the plain lawn square to her nose. While the carriage rattled over the wet cobbled streets, continuing on its way from Chelsea Bridge toward Mayfair, another idea occurred to her. What if the man took her for a Bedlamite? Who could blame him if he did? He had no reason to trust the seriousness of her mission, and chances were he would not even listen to her plea. He might take one look at her and have his butler call the watch to drag her away.

Eugenia was still struggling with that rather daunting possibility when the driver of the hackney turned the plodding horse right at Hyde Park and traversed north on

Park Lane for a matter of minutes. Once he bore right onto Upper Grosvenor Street, the jarvey reined in the animal, outside an unpretentious, yet well-kept brick town house.

Now that she was here at last, at the home of Mr. Nathaniel Seymour, Eugenia's heart began to race inside her chest like a hamster in a round cage, and she was in a fair way of convincing herself to turn around and return to her dreary little room at the Misses Becknell's Academy for Young Females. It was at the small village school south of the Thames, where she was an instructress in fine needlework, deportment, and use of the globe that she had first decided upon this fool's errand.

Staring up at the delicate wrought iron balconies on the upper floors of the narrow town house, Eugenia voiced a final animadversion upon her own intelligence. "I am an imbecile," she said. It was no more than the truth, for who but an imbecile would come out in the rain to beg favors of one of London's most renowned scoundrels.

"This be it, miss," the jarvey called from his place on the box. When she did not move, he said, "You gettin' out?"

"Yes, yes," she replied before she lost her nerve completely. "Of course I am."

"That'll be three and six, if you please."

Eugenia counted out the silver coins and handed them up to the driver, who waited only until she stepped onto the pavement before giving his tired horse a clicking signal to be on its way. The animal's bridle jingled, and soon the wheels of the hackney were rattling into the distance, leaving Eugenia standing alone before the home of a man who had no knowledge of her existence.

Of course, until last evening when her cousin Thaddeus came to call upon her, threatening to toss himself from the Tower of London, Eugenia had no more knowledge of Mr. Seymour than he had of her. Recalling her cousin's impassioned pleas for help, and knowing she could not allow him to be ruined by his own ill-advised behavior—a behavior, he had pointed out, that was partly her fault—Eugenia squared her shoulders and hurried up the three rain-soaked stone steps to the wide oak door and the protection of the small porch.

Her gloved hand shook just the least bit when she lifted the highly polished brass knocker and let it fall. The sharp sound echoed inside the building, and within less than a minute a very proper butler, dressed in modern black and wearing his own salt-and-pepper hair, opened the door. It was obvious from the way the middle-aged minion gazed at her, his eyes grown wide with surprise, that he had not expected to find a female upon the doorstep of a gentleman's residence, especially not one dressed in a nondescript brown pelisse and an equally unimpressive chip straw bonnet.

"Yes?" he asked haughtily. "How may I help you?"

Knowing better than to let a servant intimidate her, Eugenia lifted her chin. "Good morning," she replied pleasantly. "Is this the home of Mr. Nathaniel Seymour?"

The butler inclined his head.

"I should like to see Mr. Seymour upon a matter of business. Please inform him that Miss—"

"I do not believe Mr. Seymour is receiving at the moment, madam. Perhaps if you leave your card, he will return your visit later in the day."

Eugenia did not possess a supply of visiting cards, and even if she had, she doubted a man of Nathaniel Seymour's reputation would bestir himself to cross the river to visit an unknown female at the Misses Becknell's school. "I . . . I have forgotten my card case, but I should be quite happy to wait upon Mr. Seymour's convenience." She pointed to a gold brocade bench just inside the pale green-and-ivory, marble-tiled vestibule. "I could sit right there."

The butler lifted his nose as if affronted by the suggestion. "I cannot say if Mr. Seymour will be down at all today. Therefore, if you will be so good as to stand away from the door so that I may—"

"Riddle?" called a masculine voice from just inside the front room, "if that is Mr. Winfield, show him in immediately, for I am heartily bored with my own company."

The butler turned and walked to the door that was slightly ajar, pushing it all the way open to reveal a few feet of handsome willow green-and-gold Axminster carpet. "It is not Mr. Winfield, sir, but a person I believe unacquainted with yourself. She said it was a matter of business, but—"

"She?" asked the deep voice. "The *person* is a female?"

Eugenia felt heat suffuse her face, not so much from the butler's condescending reference to her as a "person," as from his master's remarking upon her gender. She might have known a man of Nathaniel Seymour's reputation would be intrigued by the information that a female was at his door. Following that realization, she grew even warmer, though she was not certain which embarrassed her more, the thought that such a man would probably expect some gilded Cyprian, or the knowledge that she was the very antithesis of one of those brightly colored ladybirds.

Fearing this might be her one opportunity to speak with the scoundrel, Eugenia swallowed whatever pride had been offended and hurried across the vestibule. Pushing past the butler, she entered what was a combination music and drawing room.

"Madam!" declared the outraged servant, "this is highly irregular." Looking at the tall, broad-shouldered man who stood beside a mahogany side table in the far corner of the room, the servant said, "Shall I call one of the footmen, sir, to escort the young woman from the premises?"

The gentleman looked up from the stack of mail he was sorting through, surprise writ plainly upon his strong, angular face. Eugenia supposed there were those who would call him handsome, for his rugged features were well proportioned, with a long, straight nose and full, well-shaped lips. Unfortunately, his skin had the bronze hue of the outdoorsman, and the contrast between his skin and his eyes was a bit startling. Those orbs were blue-gray, beneath straight light-brown brows, and to her they had a rather mysterious look.

"Mr. Seymour," she began, "if you will give me but five minutes of your time, I shall come right to the point regarding the nature of my business."

The butler caught her arm just above the elbow and gave her a tug toward the door. "This way, madam."

Eugenia yanked her arm from his grip. "Take your hands off me," she said with all the dignity she could muster. "I am not a stray dog to be tossed from the premises."

With no more than a look, the master of the house stopped the butler, who was about to lay hands upon Eugenia again. "Never mind, Riddle. I will speak with the lady."

The butler made a snorting sound that said all too clearly what he thought of females who barged into a gentleman's home, but he kept his hands to himself.

"That will be all," his employer said. "I will call you if the . . . er, stray should threaten to bite me."

Eugenia detected the tiniest twitch in the corners of that well-shaped mouth, and though she appreciated the fact that she was not to be tossed out on her ear, she took exception to his amusement at her expense.

"And now," he said, once the servant had quit the room, "what is this business you wish to discuss? Since you have seen fit to push your way into my home, I must assume the subject is of some importance, at least to you. Whether I shall find it so remains to be seen."

"Fair enough," she said, surprising him into lifting a rather sardonic brow. "I shall get right to the point, sir. I wish you to teach me how to attract the attention of a scoundrel."

Nathan Seymour was not certain he had heard the young woman correctly, especially since he had never seen a female less likely to attract the attention of any man, be he scoundrel or saint. In her brown faille pelisse and her pale blue dress that resembled nothing so much as a school mistress's uniform, she reminded him of a little brown dunnock, and like that most unobtrusive of birds, she gave the appearance of one who was quiet and retiring. As his father used to say, she looked the sort who would not say boo to a goose.

No, that was not exactly true. As Nathan looked more closely, ignoring the rain-spattered, unfashionable clothes, he noted a determination in the woman's wide brown eyes, a sort of persistence that said, "I will submit, but only so far."

Actually, they were rather nice eyes—a true brown, not that greenish mixture the poets seemed to rhapsodize about. Her hair, what he could see of it beneath the sodden bonnet, was dark brown with a reddish tint. As for her skin, that was smooth with just a hint of olive, and her profile was classical, reminding him just a bit of Urania, one of the pair of marble statues of the Muses that took pride of place in the niches on either side of the fireplace to his right.

Halting his perusal of the young woman's unremarkable appearance and focusing his attention upon her quite remarkable request, he said, "Is it possible, madam, that I misunderstood what you said? I could swear you asked me to teach you how to attract the attention of a scoundrel."

Her cheeks turned a rosy hue, as though his repeating the request rendered it embarrassing, but she nodded her affirmation. "That is what I said, sir."

"And why, if I may be allowed a moment's vulgar inquisitiveness, have you come to me? What makes you think I am the properest person to give you such advice?"

For a moment he thought she meant not to answer, but in this he was mistaken. "It was that old adage," she said.

"The adage?"

"Yes, sir. I am persuaded you know the one I mean, that if one wishes to catch a thief, 'tis best to employ the assistance of another thief."

He caught her meaning immediately, but the audacity of it so surprised him that he wanted to hear it from her own lips. Pretending to misunderstand her, he said, "Have I the right of it, madam, that you believe me to be a thief?"

What had been rosy cheeks turned the bright red of an apple. "No, sir! Not at all. I merely used the adage as an example." She cleared her throat. "Using that same logic, I concluded that it would need a scoundrel to catch a scoundrel. And . . . and I have it on good authority that you are a just such a one."

If she had been a man, Nathan might have been tempted to land her a facer; he had knocked men down for less, but her sex rendered such action wholly unacceptable. "And what, or who, gave you to understand that I am a scoundrel?"

"Thaddeus told me that you— That is, the entire town knows—" She stopped, obviously too polite to continue. "Your pardon, sir, but there seems no way to answer your question without giving offense."

"A pity, madam, that you did not think of that before."

For just an instant, those brown eyes flashed with a

show of spirit, but she swallowed whatever retort had sprung to mind. She said nothing in her own defense, and finally, Nathan said, "So, it is your wish to use one scoundrel to help you wreak havoc upon another scoundrel. Have I the right of it this time?"

She smiled, obviously relieved to discover that he was so quick. "Yes, sir. That is exactly what I wish to do."

"And what if I told you, madam, that I do not consider myself more of a scoundrel than the next fellow?"

Choosing not to look directly at him, she brushed a drop of water from the reticule that hung from her wrist. "I am persuaded that you are scoundrel enough to suit my purpose."

"High praise, indeed, madam."

The sarcasm in his voice did not go unnoticed by his visitor, whose face took on an uncertain look. "Surely what my cousin said of you is true. Are you not a hardened gambler and a womanizer?"

Here was plain speaking, indeed. Nathan was definitely a gambler, but he did not think of himself as "hardened." As for the other accusation, it was no secret that he enjoyed the fair sex; nor was the enjoyment one-sided. Be that as it may, he could hardly impart such information to a female who resembled nothing so much as a spinster governess. Instead, he said, "A wise person believes only half of what they see and almost nothing of what they hear."

She had the grace to blush. "I suppose that is good advise, only I—"

"There is something I should like to know, madam. When you came to my home uninvited and without so much as an abigail in attendance, did it not occur to you that if I were the scoundrel you believe me, I might attempt to have my way with you?"

Though her cheeks were fiery, she shook her head.

"My cousin maintained that you are a scoundrel. He said nothing of your not being a gentleman."

The absurdity of her logic struck Nathan as amusing, and he found himself hard pressed not to laugh. "A gentleman, am I? Pray, which part of being a scoundrel entitles me to that label? Are they not all villains? Blackguards? Rogues?"

"Oh, no, sir! My cousin said nothing of your being any of those things."

"You see me quite relieved," Nathan said, his words dripping with sarcasm.

"If I remember correctly," she continued, "Thad's actual words were that you are a scoundrel, but not such a one as Lord Durham."

At the mere mention of Cedric Durham's name, Nathan felt his hands ball into fists. Here was a villain, indeed, and one Nathan had reason to despise. "Am I to thank your cousin for not including me with men of Durham's ilk?"

The young woman appeared taken aback by the angry tone he could not keep from his voice. Still, she did not hesitate. "I perceive, sir, that I have blundered into something I know little about. As you can see, I am not one of the fashionable London ladies, and I have no knowledge of society and its members. When I determined to come to you for assistance, I knew I would be obliged to speak bluntly, but it was never my purpose to insult you in your own home. I beg you will forgive me."

Something about the sincerity of her apology cooled Nathan's anger. Curious as to why she had mentioned his enemy, he said, "I should like to know if Lord Durham plays a part in this scheme of yours."

"He does, sir, for he is the person I wish to attract."

Nathan just managed to keep his lip from curling in disgust. "And to what purpose would you attract his lordship?"

She took a deep breath and let it out slowly, as if this was the moment she had been dreading. "Lord Durham cheated my young cousin at cards, duping him of ten thousand pounds, which is Thad's entire inheritance. I mean to see the money returned."

"Cheated? Madam, that is a serious accusation, and one not easily forgiven. You would do well to choose a less volatile word, for though it would certainly attract his lordship's notice, I cannot think it the sort of attention you wish. The man is dangerous, far more dangerous than you know, and your being a female would not protect you from his wrath, should he decide to seek retribution."

"But retribution is exactly what *I* seek."

"You said you have no knowledge of society and its members. I agree with that assessment, madam, especially if you are under the impression that Lord Durham will return winnings earned at the gaming table."

"I am not a fool. I do not believe for an instant that he will simply hand over the money. That is why I propose to play cards with him. I plan to win back the entire ten thousand."

Keeping to himself his doubts regarding her ability to best the man at cards, Nathan said, "Durham will not sit down at the gaming table with you."

"There you are wrong, sir, for Thad tells me his lordship often plays cards with females."

"That is true enough. Those females, however, are all—" Nathan paused, not wishing to give offense.

"They are all beautiful," she finished for him. "My cousin informed me of that fact as well. His lordship plays cards with females for only one reason, because he wishes to form a liaison of sorts once the game is ended." Though she blushed, she did not stammer. "I realize that in order to bring him to the tables, I will first be obliged to charm him into wishing to seduce me."

Nathan could only stare. This somber little dunnock

expected to charm Cedric Durham—a man who considered himself a connoisseur of beautiful women? She had her work cut out for her!

Her features were good, and she possessed those dark, rather expressive eyes, but she was no beauty. Furthermore, she had neither vivacity nor youth to recommend her.

Not wishing to give voice to his doubts as to her ability to charm Durham, Nathan chose to disabuse her of the notion of challenging the scoundrel at cards. "My dear young woman, what makes you think you can succeed where your cousin failed?"

"Thad was always a poor player," she replied. "Far too impetuous to think through the game or to study his opponents' method of play. I could never teach him to use restraint. I, on the other hand, know how to bide my time until the proper moment."

"Even so, madam, I cannot think—"

"You will forgive my apparent boastfulness, Mr. Seymour, but you should know I am quite skilled at cards. No one ever bests me."

Nathan doubted the accuracy of her claim, but he merely lifted a questioning eyebrow. "You may be skilled enough to defeat your young cousin and the ladies of your acquaintance, but a man of Durham's experience is another matter entirely."

"No one bests me," she repeated quietly.

"Far be it from me to dispute a lady's word, but no matter what your skill, it is a moot point." He looked toward the door, hoping she would take the hint. "Now, if you will excuse me, madam, I must recommend that you find someone else to teach you how to lure Lord Durham to the gaming table. Believe me, I am the wrong scoundrel for the job."

"Please, sir, do not refuse me out of hand. I . . . I have a proposition to make to you." While she spoke, she dug inside her reticule and removed a small leather pouch that jingled as if filled with coins. "I understand, Mr. Seymour, that gentlemen of society never refuse a wager."

"That is a blanket generalization, madam, and one which—"

"I have more than fifty pounds here," she said, jiggling the pouch of coins. "The money is yours, sir, if you can defeat me at cards."

One look at her serious face and Nathan knew even before he asked his question what her answer would be. "And what must I wager against your fifty pounds?"

"If I win, sir, you will do as I asked. You will teach me how to be alluring enough to attract Lord Durham's notice."

Chapter Two

Later, Nathan was unable to remember what had finally convinced him to call for the cards. Perhaps he considered it the easiest way to show the foolish young woman what she would face should she be allowed to sit at the tables with any of the gentlemen of his acquaintance—gentlemen who had been pitting their skills against one another for years, and often with quite staggering wagers at stake. Or perhaps it was just that it was a dull, rainy morning, and he could not take his usual horseback ride in the park, the one activity of the day he was certain to enjoy.

As for paying visits to the homes of acquaintances, that seemed a dismal prospect. He had been in town for the better part of three months, and he had already seen and heard everyone worth seeing and hearing. Nor did he wish to seek out any of the fair sex.

Having recently divested himself of his latest mistress, leaving as his parting gift a necklace that cost him several thousand pounds, he knew that if he wished a bit of dalliance, he would be obliged either to find a new flirt or to call upon one of the young ladies who had been brought to his notice during the season. At the latter possibility, he was obliged to stifle a yawn of boredom, knowing with what girlish exuberance he would be received. Nathan Seymour might be reputed to be a scoundrel, but owing to his handsome fortune and his equally handsome estate, all but the most punctilious of the matchmaking mamas were willing to overlook his shortcomings. As it happened, he was not willing to overlook theirs.

If the truth be known, he wished nothing so much as to return to Swanleigh Hall and his estate in Hertfordshire. Unfortunately, he could not leave town for at least two weeks. He was part of the ten-member committee from White's Club responsible for the planning of the masked ball honoring the Duke of Wellington, and he could not make his escape until after the ball on July 1st.

Prinny planned a grand fete at Carlton House on July 21st, to which Nathan had been invited, and there were any number of galas and parties scheduled between that time and the first of August, when public victory celebrations were to be held in Hyde Park, Green Park, and St. James's. Nathan had already declined Prinny's invitation, and since he wanted no part of the continuing round of gaiety, he hoped to see the last of London directly after White's ball, which was to be held at Burlington House.

He was as jubilant as any other Englishman that Napoleon had been defeated, and he was grateful to know the country need sacrifice no more of her young men upon the altar of Bonaparte's mad ambition to rule the world. Still, Nathan had been from home for too long. He had drunk his fill of town and the many festivities surrounding the peace and the visiting dignitaries. As far as he was concerned, the Prince Regent, the Tsar of Russia and his sister, the Duchess of Oldenburg, King Frederick of Prussia, and even Field Marshall Blücher, that crusty, often coarse Prussian war hero who had become society's pet, could very well celebrate without Nathan Seymour's help.

Bored, idle, and wishing he were in Hertfordshire that very moment, he settled down at the square, baize-topped card table to show this misguided young woman the error of her ways. "Forgive me," he said once Riddle had taken her damp pelisse and bonnet to the kitchen to hang them by the fire, then returned with a new pack of cards and the pot of tea the woman had agreed would be most welcome, "but I seem to have forgotten your name."

"No, sir, it is I who should apologize, for I quite forgot to introduce myself. I am Miss Eugenia Bailey."

Nathan rose slightly from his chair and inclined his head. "Your servant, Miss Bailey."

While he tore open the seal from the desk and removed the crisp, unused pasteboard squares with their bright blue-and-gold fleur de lis design, he asked her where she lived.

"I was born in Surrey," she said, "near the village of Haselmere. I consider that my home, for I lived there for sixteen years, until the influenza claimed my father. Both my parents are buried at St. Anne's in Haselmere."

"And after that?" he asked quietly.

She hesitated only a moment. "Because I was still a minor, I was sent to live with the family of my father's brother. My uncle, Sir Thomas Bailey, Lady Bailey, and my cousins, Thaddeus and Alexandra, reside some twenty miles from Haselmere, at Challwith Manor, near Redgate."

"And you live there now, in your uncle's house?"

Though she gave him a look that said clearly what she thought of such impertinent questions, she finally replied. "I no longer reside with the family. After my uncle's untimely demise, I returned to the Misses Becknell's Academy for Young Females, where I had been educated. I have been there as an instructress for the past seven years."

Nathan just stopped himself from exclaiming—seven years in some third-rate female academy? No wonder she brought to mind a timid bird. Such an existence was certain to stifle the individuality of even the most colorful female. "You must have been very young when you embarked upon your career."

"If that is your subtle way of discovering my age, sir, be advised that I was nineteen when I returned to the school. Ergo, I am now six-and-twenty."

She looked him squarely in the eyes, as if to discern his reaction to the news, but as it was the very age he would have guessed her to be, he was not at all surprised.

"I realize," she continued, "that six-and-twenty is an advanced age for a lady who is only just now planning to try her hand at attracting the notice of a man of the world. Unfortunately, I cannot turn back the clock, nor would I if I could. And," she added, pushing the pouch of coins toward the middle of the table, "since I am growing older by the minute, perhaps we should begin play."

Impressed by her plain speaking, he removed the knave from the pack, returned it to the empty box, then tossed the box toward the black marble fireplace. Knowing how clumsily most females handled a deck, generally spilling cards right and left, Nathan suggested he act as dealer.

Taking her silence for acquiescence, he divided the deck, making almost a perfect center cut; then he took the halves, one in each hand, and shuffled the cards. They made a uniform *trring* sound as they intermingled; then, to add a bit of flourish, Nathan pushed upward with his fingers, ruffling the whole so they made a slightly higher pitched *trrr*. A skilled player, he normally took exception to those coxcombs who made a great show of shuffling the cards, but he thought it might be a lesson to Miss Bailey to observe the dexterity a gentleman expected at the tables.

To his surprise, she paid scant attention to his efforts. Instead, she reached her hand to the nape of her neck, where several wispy strands had worked loose from her coiffeur, obviously more interested in the order of her person than the order of the cards.

As Nathan had suspected, she had very nice hair. It was brown with reddish lights, and it showed just the slightest tendency to wave. Plainly styled, it had been brushed back from her face and fashioned into a knot atop her head, but not even that prim arrangement could dull the natural sheen of the thick tresses.

Realizing that he was staring, and not a little put out that she appeared unimpressed by his dexterity with the cards, he pushed the deck across the table to her. "I have changed my mind, Miss Bailey. Perhaps you should take the first deal."

"As you wish, sir."

The moment she took the pack in her hands, Nathan realized he had misjudged her, for she touched it with the nonchalance of one who has more than a nodding acquaintance with cards. Not even bothering to look at what she was doing, she halved the deck and began to shuffle. Her slender fingers moved lightly, and the intermingling of the cards was accomplished with the merest whisper of sound.

When they were satisfactorily mixed, she fanned them out on the table, and using the tip of her finger, she flicked the end card, causing the entire deck to rise and flip over to the left. After flipping them back to the right, she gathered up all fifty-two cards and reshuffled. "Now," she said quietly, tapping the deck to indicate that he should cut, "what shall we play? Whist? Loo? Vingt-un?"

Though Nathan silently acknowledged her dexterity, he refrained from comment. "You may choose the game you prefer."

She shook her head. "It makes not the least difference to me, sir. Therefore, the choice is yours."

"Very well," he said, making the cut, then tapping the deck as she had done, "let it be whist."

Without another word, she dealt thirteen cards to each of them, turning up the fourteenth card to designate trumps. It was a three of hearts. Since she dealt, Nathan led the first card, placing a seven of diamonds faceup on the table. Immediately, she captured it with an eight of diamonds, taking the first trick. The next three tricks were hers as well.

Confident that he could take a trick whenever he wished, Nathan used the time to study her face. Not by so much as a raised eyebrow did she give vent to her emotions. There were no girlish squeals of glee, nor even a smile when she won. As well, when he took the next two tricks in a row, her expression remained equally impassive.

The lady seized the next five tricks, and before Nathan knew it, she had won the first round.

"Not bad," he said.

"You let me win," she replied, displeasure in her tone.

Nathan was surprised by her accusation, partially because he was unaccustomed to females who questioned his actions, but mostly because he disliked the allegation. Though it was true he had not paid close attention to what he played, he certainly had not given her the round. "I assure you, Miss Bailey, I never allow anyone to win."

A flash of something in the depths of her dark eyes told Nathan she did not believe him. "If you did not purposely condescend to me because of my sex, sir, then I can only assume you are a careless player."

Not a little affronted, he said, "Upon what do you base your charge?"

"In the fourth discard, when I led clubs, you trumped with a ten. Two tricks later, you led trumps with a five."

He remembered. He had been careless in that instance, for the five of hearts had been wedged behind another card when he played the ten. "You are correct, Miss Bailey. For the error, I beg your pardon." When she said nothing more, he continued. "You appear to have a good memory. May one ask how good?"

Without another word, she gathered all the cards, shuffled them, then cut the deck as near the center as possible. She took the top half and fanned it out on the table, faces up. After concentrating on the row for several seconds, she gathered it up and put it aside. "Now," she said, "if you will take up the other half of the deck, holding the cards so I cannot see them, I will tell you what is in your hand. Please discard each card I call correctly."

Nathan did as she asked, fanning the cards in his hand. "I am ready, Miss Bailey."

"You have only the one ace," she began, "and that is in clubs, so I will begin with the deuces and work my way up to the kings."

She named each card he held, without once miscalling a value or a suit, and by the time she named the final card, the king of spades, Nathan was convinced. "I confess, madam, that I have never seen anything like that before. Allow me to inform you that your talents are wasted as an instructress."

"I pray you are wrong, sir, for I like what I do."

It was not the entire truth, of course, but Eugenia saw no reason to divulge that piece of information to someone so obviously wealthy he could never understand the few choices available to a female who must support herself. She liked teaching well enough, especially when that rare student came along who really wished to learn, but she was far from content to spend the rest of her life in the cramped attic room allotted her at the Misses Becknell's Academy. What she really wished to do was set up a small school of her own—a school for village girls who wished to better their situation in life.

Like all young females, Eugenia had once hoped to

find a man she could love—a man who would love her in return—and once she had found him, she had meant to devote her life to him and to their children. Unfortunately, she had been obliged to abandon that dream bit by tiny bit with each year she spent sequestered at the Misses Becknell's, isolated from any society but that of her students and the two elderly spinster sisters. Now, of course, there was but a trace of the dream left, and what remained of it she kept hidden deep within her heart, lest anyone discover her secret and make sport of it and her.

Not wanting to linger on such thoughts, she pushed the deck toward Mr. Seymour. "Your deal, I believe."

Two hours later, after they had completed two rubbers of whist, both of which Eugenia won, they changed to loo. Eugenia won that as well. Vingt-un was not quite so easy, for she allowed him to be the dealer, but she finally prevailed in that as well.

"Uncle!" Mr. Seymour said at last, pushing his chair back and rising from the table. He walked over to the window that looked out onto the rain-soaked street, and there he stood for quite five minutes, not moving, not speaking. Finally, as if he had come to a decision, he turned back and looked at Eugenia. "Very well, Miss Bailey, you have won your wager, and I am prepared to make good my losses. It remains only for you to tell me just how far you are prepared to go in your bid to attract Lord Durham's attention."

"You did what!" Mr. Martin Winfield all but shouted. "Nate, old boy, you must have taken leave of your senses. There can be no other explanation for such unparalleled lunacy."

Though Mr. Winfield was quite a slender gentleman, fully six inches shorter than his dinner host, and more given to poetry than to sport, he spoke without fear of reprisal from the noted Corinthian. They had been best

friends since their first year at Eton, and from the beginning of their friendship Nathan had figured as the smaller
boy's protector from the school bullies. "Send the girl
packing," the gentleman said, reaching for the brandy decanter that stood on the rosewood piecrust table just to
the right of his chair.

"Six-and-twenty is hardly a girl," Nathan said quietly.

"Whatever her age, give her the ten thousand from your
own pocket if you must, but do not take her into
your home. Mark my words, old boy, if you do this thing,
you will rue the day."

"I already rue it." Nathan put his own glass down on
the mantel and turned to stare at the niche where the
Muse Urania stood, a globe of the world balanced in her
palm. "But what can I do, Winny? This is no less a debt
of honor than if I had played with you and lost."

Winfield rolled his eyes heavenward. "As if you had
ever lost to me. And now I think of it, how the deuce did
you come to lose to a female? Were you in your cups?"

"No, I have not that excuse. I was bored; otherwise I
would not have been so foolish as to call for the cards. As
for how I came to lose to the woman, I will let *you* challenge her. A picture is worth a thousand words."

"Thank you all the same, old boy, but I've not got your
deep pockets. And if I spend so much as another groat before Quarter Day, I shall have the tradesmen dunning me.
Besides, you know how distracted I become in the presence of a pretty woman."

"On that score, at least, you would be safe, for the lady
is little more than passable."

Martin Winfield could only stare. In the dozen or so
years since he and Nathan had begun to notice the fair
sex, his friend had never been seen with a woman who
was not an incomparable. Beautiful women just seemed
to gravitate toward him. And it was not just because he
was wealthy. Unlike himself, Nathan was tall and muscu-

lar, and possessed the kind of rugged good looks the
ladies seemed to find irresistible.

As for the less virtuous females, they practically fell
into his friend's bed. Why, there was not a ladybird in the
entire town who would not pass up a duke in favor of
Nathan Seymour. In fact, at least one duke had wed one
of Nathan's discarded mistresses. Not that there was anything so very remarkable in that; half the gentlemen of
their acquaintance drew lots to see who would be next to
offer protection to Nathan's latest lightskirt.

"Let me see if I have the right of this, Nate. The lady
is not a beauty, and she is no longer in her first blush of
youth, yet she wishes you to help her attract some fellow
into playing cards with her so she can fleece him of ten
thousand pounds. Would you please explain to me why
you did not send her packing when she first stated her
reason for coming?"

For a minute Winfield thought he had crossed the line,
for his friend's mouth became hard with anger, and his
gray eyes appeared as cold as the North Sea.

"Sorry, old man," he hurried to say. "Did not mean to
pry. Naturally, whatever you decide to do is your own
business. Pray forgive—"

"The long and short of it, Winny, is the identity of the
man she wishes to attract." If possible, his voice was even
colder than his eyes. "It is Lord Durham," he said. "Miss
Bailey wishes to be revenged on Cedric Durham."

"The devil, you say!"

Chapter Three

Wednesday morning was as beautiful and sunny as the previous day had been dreary, yet Eugenia felt unaccountably dispirited. Generally truthful to a fault, she had been obliged to invent a story to explain her absence to the elder Miss Becknell, who was her friend as well as her mentor. Afraid to say she was going to Surrey, in case her cousin Thad should show up again looking for her, she had told her employer that she was to visit with a distant cousin for three or four weeks so they might take part in some of the victory celebrations going on in London.

To Eugenia's further discomfort, the elderly lady had been happy for her young protégée. "A bit of fun is just what you need," Miss Agnes had said. "If I were thirty years younger, I should be joining in the celebrations myself."

Eugenia had not allowed Mr. Seymour to send his own coach to fetch her, as he had suggested, for a grand conveyance would have occasioned comment, but she had readily agreed to his sending a hackney carriage. The jarvey had arrived in good time, and once he had stowed Eugenia's trunk atop the coach, she climbed in and waved farewell to Miss Agnes.

The trip across Chelsea Bridge seemed to pass all too quickly, and before Eugenia had time to prepare herself mentally for this insane undertaking, the hackney rattled to a stop outside Mr. Seymour's Grosvenor Square town house. Her knees shook at the prospect of entering the elegant establishment once again—and with good reason. Yesterday the butler had looked down his nose at her for merely calling upon a bachelor; what would he think to see her arrive with a trunk?

Worse still, what would the world think? Of course, she knew the answer to that question. The world would think she was Nathaniel Seymour's mistress.

"I cannot remain here!" she had told him yesterday when he made the suggestion that she come there on the morrow so they could begin her instruction.

"Of course you can," he said replied. "Did you think to go back to the Misses Buckfaces each day?"

"Becknell," she corrected. "As to that, sir, I fear I did not give the matter much thought."

"There appear to be quite a number of things to which you have not given sufficient thought. You still have not told me how far you are prepared to go in your bid to get Lord Durham to the gaming table."

"I am prepared to do all that is necessary to attract his attention."

An unholy light had shown in those cool gray eyes. "*All* that is necessary? Are you prepared to cross that subtle line between attracting a man's attention and displaying a sort of blatant voluptuousness?"

"I—"

"Believe me," he said, not allowing her to answer his question, "Cedric Durham will definitely respond to voluptuousness. The question remains, are *you* willing to respond to his possible suggestion of a quick tumble in the hay?"

"Sir! You know I am not!" Eugenia felt a flush spread up her neck to burn in her face. She knew what Nathan Seymour was doing—he was trying to shock her into giving up the scheme. "I seek only one thing, to win back my cousin's ten thousand."

"Without crossing that subtle line?"

"Without crossing it," she replied. "After the game has been played and the money returned to my cousin, I will be obliged to resume my former life. I cannot do so if my reputation is in shreds."

"Very well, madam. Be warned, however, for subtlety is much harder to teach than voluptuousness. The lessons will be lengthy and time is short, for I do not mean to remain in town for more than two weeks. For that reason, you must come here."

"I told you, sir, I cannot stay in this house."

He had refused to argue the point, and in time she had agreed to remove to Grosvenor Square. Unfortunately, though she knew within her heart that she was doing only what had to be done, that knowledge did not make it any easier to face the butler's obvious disapproval.

"Mr. Seymour had an appointment at his club," Riddle informed her, his tone decidedly icy, "but as he instructed, a room has been prepared for you. This way, if you please."

The butler turned then, and, traversing the pale green and ivory marble tiles of the vestibule, he made his way past the gold brocade bench and a cherry console table, his destination the polished oak staircase that gave access to the upper floors. Eugenia followed him; she had no recourse but to do so, though she had never wanted anything so much as she wanted to run back outside, hail the hackney, and bid the jarvey return her to the school.

She passed the ground-floor drawing room, where she had played cards with Nathan Seymour yesterday; it was handsomely decorated in shades of celadon green and gold, and it ran almost the complete width of the town house. The upper-floor drawing room, however, was far less formal and was only half the width of the house.

Done in cream and blue, it, too, faced the street, as did the bedchamber just beyond. It was this room to which Riddle showed Eugenia.

"That," he said, indicating the door opposite her own, "is the master bedchamber."

Eugenia thought her face might burst into flame. So, the butler did believe she was here to be Nathan Seymour's ladybird. Not that she could blame him. Mr. Seymour might say he would do all within his power to keep her identity a secret so this escapade did not get back to either her family or her employers, but there was no keeping anything from the servants.

Trying for a bit of dignity, she said, "Thank you, Riddle," for all the world as though he had done her a kindness in pointing out the master bedchamber.

"Here is Fiona," he said, indicating a young girl who had just placed a brass can containing hot water upon the washstand in the corner of the pretty blue guest bedchamber. "Mr. Seymour has instructed that she is to wait upon you personally for the duration of your stay."

Astonished at this unlooked-for thoughtfulness, Eugenia thanked both the butler and the serving girl, who could not have been more than twelve, about the age of Eugenia's students. The maid bobbed her an awkward curtsy, but Riddle merely inclined his head and backed himself out of the room, not bothering with a further show of politeness.

Before Eugenia could recover from that snub, a pair of tall, dark-haired footmen appeared at the door, carrying her trunk. "Set it on the floor beside the bed," she instructed.

"Shall I see to the straps for you, miss?" one of the footmen asked.

"No, thank you. I will do it later." She remembered just in time that the footmen might expect a gratuity, so she reached inside her reticule and withdrew two coins, placing a sixpence in each man's hand. Both men touched their forelocks politely, then quit the room.

" 'Appen the guv will 'ave somefing to say about that," the maid said angrily once the door was closed.

Eugenia turned quickly, surprised both by the child's rough cockney and her vehemence. Thinking she must have committed some in-house blunder, she stared at the youngster, who was less than five feet tall and weighed scarcely five stone. Her apron was so large on her frail bones it had to be doubled at the waist to keep her from tripping on it, and her mobcap fell down on her forehead, all but obscuring her dark blond hair.

"I 'eard the guv telling Mr. Riddle as 'ow weren't nobody to take no vails from you, miss. On account of you being indignant."

If Eugenia had not been so surprised at this information, she might have laughed. "I daresay Mr. Seymour said I was 'indigent,' which is not exactly true. I am employed at a school for young ladies, and though I must work to support myself, I am not totally without funds."

"Coo ee!" the youngster said, her blue eyes big as saucers. "You must be one of them smart morts. Can you read and everyfing, miss?"

Though not certain what "everything" entailed, Eugenia nodded.

"Coo ee!"

Fiona may have been small, but she was neat and methodical, and in no time she had Eugenia's trunk unpacked with the plain lawn underthings folded neatly and placed in the rosewood chest of drawers and the few meager dresses hung in the big oak chiffonnier. She talked nonstop while she worked, and in no time Eugenia knew the youngster's history. Orphaned and homeless, she had gone to the workhouse—a place she hoped never to see again even if she lived to be a hundred—and only this

spring had she been brought here to work for Mr. Seymour, the guv, as she called him.

"And 'e told Mr. Riddle I was to be treated fair, the guv
did, and not worked too 'ard, and fed 'til I couldn't eat no
more." The loquacious youngster patted her flat belly and
smiled wickedly. "I still got some fattening up to do, but
I'm doing me best by Mrs. Drockett's cooking."

A knock at the door finally silenced the child, and
though Eugenia would have liked to ask how Mr. Seymour came to hire her, she kept her curiosity to herself.
"Come in," she called.

It was one of the footmen. "Begging your pardon,
miss, but Mr. Creel said to inform you that Mr. Seymour
has returned home, and that he would like to see you in
the small drawing room in ten minutes."

As soon as the servant left, Eugenia asked Fiona who
Mr. Creel might be.

" 'E's the guv's varlet," she replied.

"Ah, yes," Eugenia said, only just hiding her smile.

Crossing the room to the dresser and the small looking
glass just above it, she made certain her hair was neat,
with no stray tresses falling from the topknot. She had
chosen to travel in her best frock, an olive green muslin,
but she was obliged to adopt a fichu to conceal the swell
of bosom revealed by the frock's square neck. After
straightening the plain lawn, she bid Fiona farewell and
took herself to the drawing room to await her new instructor.

Mr. Seymour did not keep her waiting above a minute,
and when he entered the room, Eugenia had only just disposed herself on the pretty cream settee with its wide blue
stripes and was admiring the subtle blend of colors. One
look at the gentleman, however, and all thoughts of the
decoration of the room left her head.

The man looked splendid!

She had been too nervous the day before to give full attention to Nathan Seymour's clothing, and though she was only slightly less nervous today, at least she was calm enough to note how well his clothes suited his physique and his coloring. His dove gray coat was worn over a sky blue waistcoat and gray pantaloons, and while the waistcoat gave a hint of blue to his gray eyes, the dove gray of the coat perfectly suited his tanned skin and his light brown hair.

He gave her olive green muslin a cursory glance, but if he was as enchanted by what he saw as she had been by her view of him, he kept the information to himself.

"You arrived in good time," he said, "I presume that means you still wish to follow through with this plan to attract Lord Durham's attention."

"It does, sir."

"So be it then."

Nathan did not close the drawing room door, but pulled a lyre-back chair quite close to the settee, where they could speak privately. "To begin with, I have been thinking how best to ensure that you leave here with your reputation intact, and I have two suggestions to make. The first is that we keep your full name a secret. With that in mind, I propose to call you Eugenia."

He paused to see if this met with her approval. When she said nothing, he continued. "You, of course, must call me Nathan. Otherwise, there is no way we can convince Lord Durham that you and I are, uh, friends."

When she lowered her eyes, he muttered something beneath his breath. "Deuce take it, Miss Bai—Eugenia, if we are to accomplish your objective, we must do it properly. And," he added, "no matter how embarrassing you may find my instructions, I insist that you follow them to the letter, without argument and without treating me to a display of missishness."

She lifted her chin rather stubbornly, as if she meant to

take umbrage with his tone. She said nothing, however, merely gave him look for look.

Taking her silence for agreement, he continued. "My second suggestion to ensure that your reputation is not irreparably harmed is that you never show your entire face while in public. This should not be too difficult to accomplish. A partial veil, or a cleverly held parasol—"

"Must I be that much in the public eye? I had hoped to encounter as few people as possible."

Nathan shook his head. "It cannot be helped. Because Lord Durham has shown a tendency, in the past, to admire those ladies living under my protection, your appearing to be my newest *inamorata* will whet his appetite."

At the word *inamorata*, she lowered her eyes, but she remained true to her promise and displayed no further missishness.

"To put this idea of our liaison in his lordship's mind, you and I will be seen riding through the park on one or two occasions, occasions in which I will purposefully *not* introduce you to anyone."

"Will that be enough, do you think?"

"No, but an air of mystery is always a good beginning. We will follow that with an appearance at Burlington House. White's is sponsoring a masked ball there a week from Friday. It is a victory celebration, and everyone will be there, Durham included. If I know the fellow, he will find a way to force my hand so that I will have no recourse but to introduce him to you."

"A week from Friday? But . . . but that is only eleven days from now."

"I believe it is so, but what has that to say to the matter?"

Her hand went to the hair at the nape of her neck, a gesture Nathan was beginning to recognize as a show of nervousness. "I do not own a ball gown, sir, and though

I am proficient with a needle, I cannot think eleven days would be time enough for me to make anything suitable."

"It is of no consequence," he said, "for I have arranged for an acquaintance of mine—a friend of long standing—to see to your clothing. She knows exactly what you will need."

She? An inamorata, perhaps?

"You will oblige me by putting yourself completely in her hands."

For a moment, it passed through Eugenia's mind that this entire scheme was pure madness. Before she could voice as much to him, however, she heard herself say, "I will do as you ask, Mr. Seymour, and—"

"Nathan," he said. "You must remember to call me by my name."

"I will remember . . . Nathan. And I thank you for your assistance."

"A gentleman always pays his debts of honor."

With that, he stood and stepped toward the door, though he paused just inside the threshold. "I will leave you for now, Eugenia, but I will expect to meet you again at dinner. My friend, Mr. Martin Winfield, will join us for the meal; then he and I will take ourselves off. It being midsummer night, Winny and I have plans for the evening, plans that could not be broken at this late date."

"No, no. Of course not. I should not wish to interfere with your plans."

He made her a slight bow. "Until dinner."

"Sir," she called, stopping him just at the door. "You did not mention it, but since you seem to have thought of everything else, have you plans for when I might get Lord Durham to the tables?"

"I have. It will be an evening party for gentlemen only, with perhaps one or two members of the fair sex invited to join us so that your attendance will occasion less comment."

"And the date?"

"We will select the date this evening. Because so many fetes are scheduled for the next two months, we must choose wisely to ensure that our little gathering will not be overshadowed by some more elevated affair. Mr. Winfield is making a list of all the proposed parties and will bring it with him."

"But what of Lord Durham? How can we be certain he will attend the party?"

A look crossed Nathan Seymour's handsome face, a look so filled with anger it sent a chill down Eugenia's back. "Have no fear, madam, Lord Durham will come. If nothing else, the novelty of an invitation from me will guarantee his attendance. Once he is here, however, my part in the scheme will be finished and yours will begin. It will be left to you to entice him into testing his skills against yours."

From the coolness in his voice, Eugenia suspected that her teacher held out little hope of her success, and for just a moment she shared his misgivings. Once he quit the room, however, her faith in herself returned. After all, this was not the first time she had been faced with a task that seemed beyond her ability.

At the age of sixteen, orphaned and with little more than a token inheritance—an inheritance she could not touch until she gained her majority—Eugenia had been obliged to make her home with the family of her Uncle Thomas. From the onset, she had been made to feel as though she were a charity case, one who should be eternally grateful for the very food on her plate. Though she tried to earn her keep by making herself useful to her aunt and to her young cousins, her efforts were never enough. Lady Bailey could not be pleased.

After Sir Thomas's death, the situation grew worse. Within a fortnight of her uncle's funeral, her aunt began to hint that supporting a plain and dowerless, therefore unmarriageable, relative was a severe drain upon the finances of the estate. When Eugenia could no longer ignore the remarks, she vowed to leave Challwith Manor even if she starved to death in the hedgerows.

Though she was poorly equipped for employment, she was determined to make her own way in the world. Not wanting to remain with her aunt a moment longer than was necessary, she wrote a letter to her friend Miss Agnes Becknell, asking for advice. Five days later, a letter arrived from Miss Agnes offering Eugenia employment as an assistant instructress at the school. Though the salary was but fifteen pounds per annum—wages on a par with those of a kitchen maid's—Eugenia packed her trunk immediately, promising herself never to return to Redgate.

Though the next seven years had been difficult, Eugenia had worked hard and risen to a position as full instructress with a salary of thirty pounds per annum. If hers was not a glorious career, at least she was beholden to no one, and she had proven to herself that she could do whatever was necessary.

"And," she said aloud, "nothing will stop me from enticing that scoundrel, Lord Durham, to the gaming table. Nothing. I will have that ten thousand!"

Somewhere, just below the thin veneer of adulthood, lay a young girl's remembered humiliation at having been a poor relation, unwanted and barely tolerated. Now Eugenia had a chance to expunge that memory, and no matter what was required of her, nothing would prevent her from winning back that ten thousand pounds.

Once she had the money, she would return to Challwith Manor one last time. She would stand before her aunt, fan the pound notes in her hand so Lady Bailey could see them clearly, then she would toss them on the floor like so much trash.

"There!" she would say. "Never let it be said that Eugenia Bailey did not pay her debts."

With that vision of vindication strengthening her resolve, she rose from the settee and traversed the short
corridor to the room next door. Thankfully, she found the
bedchamber empty, for she needed some time alone. Because she had been too nervous to sleep the night before,
she turned back the handsome blue counterpane and lay
down upon the feather mattress. Almost the moment her
head touched the pillow, she fell asleep.

What seemed like only minutes later, Eugenia heard a
voice call to her from some cavernous, echoing place.
She moaned, not wanting to forsake the pleasure of such
blissful sleep.

"Miss," the voice insisted, "you'd best be opening
your peepers, on account of the guv ain't one as likes to
be kept waiting."

Eugenia obeyed the command and opened her eyes,
looking directly into Fiona's worried face. The child was
mere inches from her and was shaking her shoulder. It
seemed the little Cockney was taking her new position as
lady's maid seriously.

"What time is it?" Eugenia asked.

"Near about time for dinner, miss. Best shake a leg if you
don't want to keep the gentlemen waiting. I pressed your
dress, and I've brought 'ot water so you can make your ab-
solutions."

"Ablutions," Eugenia corrected sleepily.

She had slept for several hours, and now she stretched
languidly, enjoying the luxury of the spacious, soft bed
and the sensuous feel of fine linen sheets against her skin.
Though she would have liked to savor the moment, she
heard Fiona pour the water into the washbowl, then
arrange the dressing screen for privacy, and she knew she
must get up. The little maid was correct; she should not
keep Mr. Seym—no, Nathan—and his friend waiting.

Eager to know the date of the card party, Eugenia
washed herself, then brushed through her long, thick

locks and arranged them atop her head. Feeling just a bit daring, she did not pull the hair straight back in her usual style, but arranged it more loosely, letting the natural waves fall where they might. As if to show their appreciation, the undulating tresses caressed the tops of her ears, drawing attention to the feminine curve of her jaw.

Rather pleased with the effect, she allowed Fiona to help her into her good dinner dress, the pale gold sarcenet she saved for those rare occasions when she and the Misses Becknell treated themselves to a concert or an evening at the theater. The gown, sewn by her own hands, would probably be scorned by a wealthy society miss, but it was the nicest Eugenia had ever owned, and just the feel of the soft sarcenet always lifted her spirits. As well, the gold complemented her skin tones and brought out the red highlights in her hair.

"Oh, miss," Fiona said, "you look a picture, you do."

"Thank you." Never a vain female, Eugenia was nonetheless pleased not to look a complete dowd for her first dinner alone with a gentleman. Two gentlemen, she reminded herself quickly, lest she delude herself into thinking Mr. Nathaniel Seymour had asked her to dine with him for any other reason than to get down to business.

As she took one last look in the glass, she touched the suggestion of rounded bosom that showed above the unadorned square neckline of the dress, wishing, not for the first time, that she possessed a necklace of some kind to break up the wide expanse of bare shoulders and chest. Since she had no such finery, she thanked Fiona for her help, then hurried down the staircase to the ground floor, where one of the footmen opened the door to the front drawing room.

"Good evening," she said to Nathan Seymour, who stood beside the black marble mantel, a glass of sherry in his hand. "After we spoke this afternoon, sir, I returned to my room, where the demands of the past twenty-four hours finally caught up with me, prompting me to fall asleep. If I have kept you waiting, I hope you will forgive my unpunctuality."

Her host said not a word; he merely looked her over from head to toe, his gaze lingering for a moment on her bare shoulders and the swell of her bosom. Though he turned away to set his glass upon the mantel, effectively masking his reaction to her appearance, Eugenia had intercepted a look of surprise in his eyes. More pleased than insulted by that look, she smiled pleasantly and curtsied to him.

"Good evening," said an elegantly dressed stranger who had stood at her entrance, set his glass of sherry upon a rosewood table, then made her a very courtly bow. "You are not at all unpunctual, ma'am, but allow me to inform you that it would not matter if you were. Some things are worth the wait."

The dark-haired gallant was a smallish man, quite slender and barely taller than Eugenia, but he possessed a warm, infectious smile that lit his blue eyes. Responding to his warmth, Eugenia could not help but return his smile. "You are very kind, sir."

"Not at all," the gentleman said, coming forward to accept the hand she extended. "I understand that I am not to use your last name."

"No, sir, but I should be pleased if you would call me Eugenia."

"You are very gracious," he said, lifting her fingers to his lips. "Since our host seems to have misplaced whatever manners he may possess, allow me to introduce myself. I am Martin Winfield."

"Mr. Winfield," she said.

"As we are to be co-conspirators, as it were, may I hope, ma'am, that you will agree to call me Winny?"

She looked to Nathan for confirmation, but when he

still said nothing, she returned her attention to Mr. Winfield. "Winny it is," she said.

Having refused the offer of a glass of sherry, Eugenia disposed herself upon the celadon green settee, folded her hands in her lap, and waited for Nathan Seymour to introduce the topic of the card party.

It was left to Nathan's friend to pave the way. "So," Mr. Winfield began, "you are to charm Lord Durham."

"It is my *hope* to charm him, sir. The achievement is by no means a certainty."

She glanced quickly at the drawing room door to assure herself that the footman had closed it behind him. He had. Confident now that the three of them were alone, she said, "Unfortunately, my skills at flirtation are unhoned, and I fear I have no experience with the give and take between the sexes." She felt her face grow warm at the admission. "I have been little in society. Other than attending one or two of the assemblies in Redgate, under the watchful eyes of my aunt, my experience is limited to the occasional concert or theater party."

"Ah, yes, the theater. 'The play's the thing,'" quoted the gentleman, effectively smoothing over Eugenia's confession of social inexperience. "The theater is my favorite pastime, ma'am. In fact, I hold it to be one of the few truly civilized enjoyments of society."

"To be sure," Nathan Seymour agreed, speaking at last, "quite civilized. Especially when the groundlings become angry and throw rotting vegetables at the actors upon the stage."

"Ignore him," Mr. Winfield bid her, "for Nate was ever a Philistine."

Eugenia looked to see how their host had taken such a slur, and to her surprise, his lips twitched as if he tried to suppress a smile. "Have a care, Winny, or when next we are at the theater, vegetables might not be the only thing tossed onto the stage."

Mr. Winfield appeared not the least concerned for his safety. "Idle threats, old man. Idle threats."

Dismissing his host's warning, he gave his attention back to Eugenia. "If I may be so bold, Miss Eugenia, may I hope that once this Durham business is at an end, I might have the honor of escorting you, and the Misses Becknell, of course, to Covent Garden? It is my favorite theater."

"Mine, too, sir. And yes, the ladies and I should be very pleased to accept your escort."

At that moment, Riddle opened the door to announce that dinner was served, and Mr. Winfield smiled again and offered Eugenia his arm. "May I?" he asked.

This time she did not look to Nathan for endorsement of her actions, merely took Mr. Winfield's proffered arm. Just before they quit the drawing room, however, she glanced over her shoulder at Nathan. His handsome brow was marred by a scowl of annoyance. Eugenia could not say which of them had been the cause of his vexation, but she suspected it might have been his old friend, the very charming Mr. Winfield.

Chapter Four

Eugenia enjoyed the dinner immensely, for Mr. Winfield seemed to go out of his way to ensure that it was a pleasant affair and that she was made to feel comfortable. In that, he succeeded, for within a very short time she felt as though she had known the gentleman for years.

"The most advantageous date," he said, lifting a forkful of haricot in oyster sauce to his mouth, "is the fortnight following White's ball. I have received one or two invitations for the fifteenth, but nothing to signify. If you choose that evening, Nate, you should have no trouble filling your tables."

Nathan gave the matter a moment's thought, then he said, "The fifteenth it is. I had hoped to return to Hertfordshire immediately after the ball, for there are some matters that require my attention. However, if it cannot be, then—"

"Oh, please," Eugenia interrupted. "Do not let this keep you from your estates. I can quite easily remain here while you are gone. Or," she added without enthusiasm, "I can return to the school. Of course, that would necessitate my inventing another falsehood the night of the card party, but—"

"If I go to Hertfordshire," Nathan said with finality, "you will go with me. We can continue our lessons as easily there as here."

"The very thing," Mr. Winfield said. "Perhaps I shall pay you a visit there. A very pretty place, Swanleigh Hall. We could take a stroll down to the lake, where I could show you the famous black swans from which the estate gets its name."

"You are very kind, sir, but I cannot—"

"We will all go to Swanleigh," Nathan said, his tone far from gracious. "Now, let me hear no more upon the subject."

Eugenia had no idea what had precipitated Nathan's displeasure, but *she* would certainly have more to say later on the subject of Hertfordshire. She had come to Nathan Seymour for assistance, not to be ordered about like one of his lackeys. For now, worried that she might give voice to her annoyance, she decided it might be a good time to leave the gentlemen to their port.

The decision made, she set her napkin beside the gold-edged dinner plate and rose from the table. Immediately, both men stood as well. "I shall bid you both good evening," she said, "and wish you an enjoyable Midsummer's Eve."

Mr. Winfield came around the table to escort her from the room. "I hope the revelers on the street do not intrude upon your rest, Miss Eugenia."

While the footman held the door open, Mr. Winfield bowed over Eugenia's fingers and bid her a good evening. "Until we meet again, ma'am."

"Until then," she replied. After politely nodding toward Nathan, she quit the room.

To her surprise, she found the vestibule empty. Since there was not a servant in sight, she walked over to the cherry console table, upon which reposed a brace of candles, took up one of the single candlesticks, and lit the taper to show her the way up the stairs and to the bed-chamber. Her foot had just touched the bottom-most riser when she heard voices coming from the dining room.

Someone had left the door ajar, and though Eugenia had not intended to eavesdrop, she paused when she heard her name spoken.

"What the deuce are you about, Winny, making such a cake of yourself?"

Eugenia clutched the newel post, for Nathan was clearly irritated.

"A cake of myself? Whatever do you mean, old boy?"

"You know damned well what I mean." When he spoke again, his voice was derisive and obviously meant to mimic his friend's. " 'I will show you the swans! May I escort you to the theater!' Deuce take it, Winny, she is a—"

"A very pleasant lady," Mr. Winfield interrupted, "and certainly more than 'passable-looking' as you described her earlier."

Eugenia's hand shook, and she nearly spilled the lighted candlestick. It was not so much that she rated her own beauty highly, it was just that she found it daunting to hear herself described as "passable-looking." Nathan might as well have called her an antidote and been done with it!

"I can understand, Nate, that she might not live up to your exacting standards of female beauty, but mine are far more lenient. To own the truth, I found her quite pretty. Furthermore, she is intelligent. I like intelligent women."

There was a bark of laughter. "Since when?"

"My mother is intelligent," Mr. Winfield replied, his tone affronted. "If the truth be known, Mother is quite the bluestocking, and you cannot deny that she and I get on famously."

"I cannot deny that Lady Winfield is devoted to you, Winny, but I never noticed that she spent much time in serious conversation with you. And only think how she and your father argue. Politics, literature, even the running of the estate, they are forever on opposite sides of any given topic. Is that what you want?"

There was silence for a moment. When Mr. Winfield answered, the animosity was gone from his voice. "I merely asked the lady if I might take her to a play. An unexceptional invitation, I assure you."

"And it was very gallant of you, Winny, but she is a schoolmistress—a spinster well past any hope of marriage—and by her own admission she is not privy to the ways of society. I think you would do better not to encourage her to believe your invitations might lead to something more serious. Once the card party is a thing of the past, I am persuaded it would be wisest to let the lady return to that sphere to which she belongs."

"The sphere to which she belongs." Eugenia was torn between anger and humiliation. It was true what was said of eavesdroppers, for they did, indeed, hear ill of themselves.

She wished she had never lingered. Not only had she learned that Mr. Nathan Seymour considered her looks no more than passable, but she had also been put soundly in her place. He had called her a spinster, which though unpalatable was no more than the truth, but she could have wished he had left off the part about her being past any hope of marriage. Of course, it was equally truthful that she was not a society lady, and that she never would be. She was a teacher in a second-rate school, and no matter how she might tell herself otherwise, that was her sphere.

What had been a pleasant dinner was now overshadowed by mortification, and Eugenia hurried up the stairs, eager to find the privacy of her bedchamber before the tears that stung her eyes spilled over and coursed their way down her cheeks. Unfortunately, even the desired privacy was to be denied her, for when she stepped inside the darkened room, she found Fiona sound asleep upon a pallet on the floor, childlike snores reverberating in the stillness.

After the initial shock of discovering the maid, Eugenia assumed the young girl must have been told to sleep there so that she might act as a sort of chaperon. It was an unlooked-for courtesy, and Eugenia supposed she should have been grateful. Later, however, after she had removed her pretty gold sarcenet, donned her plain night rail, then crawled beneath the covers of the feather bed, she began to wonder just whose reputation the maid was there to protect. Was it Eugenia's, or was it Mr. Nathan Seymour's?

The next morning, Nathan sent word that a carriage would be awaiting her convenience at ten of the clock. Eugenia bristled, not at all misled by the polite phrasing, for she recognized an order when she heard one. Upon further reflection, however, she reminded herself that it was *she* who had asked her host for help, and not the other way around. It would be best for all concerned, she decided, if she ceased taking offense at each perceived snub and simply got on with the job for which she had come.

With that resolve, she presented herself at the front door just as the tall case clock behind the stairs sounded the hour.

"The carriage is waiting," Riddle said, opening the door for her, but not offering to escort her to the street.

Reminding herself not to take offense, Eugenia nodded politely and thanked the butler for his service. Not for the world would she ask him if the coachman had been given the proper direction. Far better to wander around London forever than to give the starched-up fellow the joy of knowing that she had not the least notion where she was bound.

As it transpired, the coachman seemed to know exactly

where he was to take her, for as soon as she climbed into the stylishly appointed landau, choosing to sit facing forward so she would be covered by the carriage's top, the single pair of grays moved away from the curb and melded with the work-a-day traffic. At that hour of the morning, the streets were filled with all manner of jostling pedestrians, as well as costermongers with their fresh fish and fruit, workmen's drays, peddlers' carts, and barrows piled high with used clothing and battered pots and pans. Even so, the journey was far more comfortable than Eugenia's previous trips in the hackney.

Within half an hour, the driver reined in the pair before a modest but well-kept town house just north of Bloomsbury. Immediately, a housemaid in a crisp apron and cap opened the door and hurried down the steps to give Eugenia a hand climbing out of the carriage. "This way, miss, if you please. Miss Parker and the others be waiting for you."

Puzzled as to who the "others" might be, yet happy to know she was expected, Eugenia followed the servant up the stone steps. After passing through a small vestibule, they climbed the carpeted stairs to a tastefully, if not lavishly, decorated sitting room.

"Miss has arrived," the maid informed the young woman who rose from a jonquil satin lady's chair. "Shall I fetch Maeve and the seamstress?"

"Please," the woman replied. "And in about an hour, have a tea tray sent up. By that time, I daresay our guest will be happy for a bit of a respite." She smiled when she said this last, and came toward Eugenia, both gloved hands outstretched in greeting. "How do you do? I am Henrietta Parker, an old friend of Nathan Seymour's, and I welcome you to my home."

Not immune to such a pleasant reception, Eugenia allowed her hands to be taken in the woman's friendly grasp. "Thank you, ma'am. You are most kind to receive me."

"Not at all," she replied. "As soon as Nathan told me what was afoot, I knew that I was the very person to assist you in the choice of your wardrobe."

Henrietta Parker was unlike any other female Eugenia had ever known. More striking than beautiful, due in part to eyes that were as blue as cornflowers and hair as black and lustrous as the wings of a magpie, she wore a peach-colored day dress that complemented both hair and eyes, as well as her clear, smooth complexion. Her figure was rather voluptuous, and as she took Eugenia toward the window so she could study her in the full light, Eugenia scrutinized her as well, discovering that her hostess was not as young as she had first appeared.

She was perhaps thirty years old, and in the bright morning light it was obvious her complexion owed much to skillfully applied powder and paint. Still, she was a most attractive female, and no one could doubt the warmth and sincerity of her nature.

She asked Eugenia to remove her bonnet so she might see her hair, then she turned her around, examining her figure from all angles. "Yes," she said at last, "you will pay for the dressing, as the saying goes. I only wish there was time to see you properly outfitted. As it is, Nathan and I have agreed that a few of my frocks, judiciously altered, should do for what you have in mind."

At that moment, there was a knock at the door, and at Henrietta's call two middle-aged females entered the room. One wore the apron and frilly cap of a lady's maid, while the other was dressed in serviceable gray bombazine with a pincushion tied to her wrist. Both women carried across their arms dozens of dresses—frocks of every color of the rainbow.

"Lay them across the settee," Henrietta instructed the women, "so the young lady and I can sort through the lot." Turning to Eugenia, she said, "With your coloring, my dear, I believe we should rule out the pastels and choose from the jewels."

Her meaning was immediately obvious as she tossed aside a creation of pale pink and another of celestial blue. "Yes," she said, laying a ruby-colored silk across Eugenia's shoulder. "This one. And most definitely these," she added, handing to the seamstress an emerald satin ball gown and a matching domino.

Next came a faille carriage dress of lapis lazuli, and after that, so many rich, vibrant colors they began to run together in Eugenia's mind. Cinnamons, coppers, golds, a Prussian blue. "Please," she said when she felt almost as if she were smothering in a mountain of satins, crepe de chines, and jaconets, "I am persuaded I could not wear half that many clothes if I remained in town for the entire summer. I know I cannot pay for even one such creation, for each must surely cost more than a year's wages."

"You are not to think of that," Henrietta assured her, "for Nathan is to stand the nonsense. And," she added with a conspiratorial wink, "for each dress you take, I am to receive a replacement of *my* choosing at Madame Celeste's on Bond Street."

"But I cannot accept clothing from Nathan Seymour!"

"Of course you can," she countered, signaling to the maid who began to unfasten the buttons of Eugenia's olive green muslin.

Eugenia moved away from the agile fingers that had all but removed her dress. "I cannot do it," she insisted. "This entire scheme was my idea, and I never meant for Nathan to do more than advise me. I *will* not allow him to expend money on my behalf."

Obviously perceiving the earnestness of Eugenia's feelings, Henrietta nodded toward the maid and the seamstress, who took themselves off, closing the door behind them. "Now," she said, her voice serious, "you will please listen to me, my dear. You must take the clothes. The plan will not work without them. Lord Durham will never believe you to be a ladybird if you do not exhibit the proper plumage."

Eugenia shook her head. "I cannot do as you wish, though I sincerely regret that you will not get your new frocks from Madame Celeste's. You will think me unpardonably missish, but—"

"No, no. Not at all. One must be true to one's convictions. I try never to judge others, for each of us must live the best we know how, desirous of doing nothing to injure others or to sabotage our own soul."

Sighing with relief, Eugenia said, "You understand then, why I feel as I do?"

"Of course, my dear. There is, however, something you should know. You are not the only person who wishes to right a wrong. Nathan has a stake in this scheme as well. He has a score of his own to settle with Lord Durham. As do I."

"You? I do not understand."

"How could you? Mine is a sordid tale, and one I take no pleasure in telling." She hesitated a moment, and from the way she bit her bottom lip, it was obvious to Eugenia that she was experiencing real distress.

"Please," Eugenia said, "you owe me no explanations. I should hate to repay your kindness by forcing you to divulge something that is clearly painful for you to recall."

"Painful? Odd you should choose such a word, for what happened to me was extremely painful."

Henrietta walked over to the jonquil lady's chair she had occupied earlier. After bidding Eugenia be seated in the companion chair, she began to unbutton the elbow-length gloves she wore. Slowly, she worked the fingers loose and inched the peach-colored kid down from her forearms, not stopping until both gloves were removed.

"See for yourself," she said, holding her hands out in front of her.

Eugenia gasped, for she could not stop the surprised reflex. The backs of the woman's hands were badly scarred, the flesh taut as though it had been burned. "Ma'am, I—"

"Actually," Henrietta said, "I was lucky. The fire destroyed my bed, but it was put out before it could spread to the remainder of the room. Thankfully, I awoke at the first scent of smoke. The draperies had been closed around the bed, then they had been set on fire. Someone had touched a flame to the velvet."

"Someone? Surely, ma'am, it was but an unfortunate accident."

Henrietta began to pull the gloves back over her hands. "The draperies were open when I went to sleep, for I never close them. From childhood I have been unable to sleep closed in."

"And . . . and you believe that someone was . . ." She could not even say the name.

"Lord Durham," Henrietta finished for her.

"But why?"

"The man is a scoundrel, but that you already know. He is also vindictive, and if he feels he has been made an object for ridicule, he will not rest until he has wreaked vengeance upon the person responsible."

She fastened first one glove then the other, taking time to fit the tiny pearl buttons into their equally small buttonholes. "Lord Durham fancied me, but I would not accept his protection, even though I had recently broken all ties with Sir M— Oh, well, that part is unimportant. What matters is that when Durham made me his final offer, it was at a party, and more than one gentleman was within hearing."

"And you refused him?"

"I did more than that. I spurned his offer. And him. I

had drunk a bit more champagne than was wise, and when he approached me, stealing a kiss and pawing me before I knew what he was about, I slapped his face. The blow was resounding, and several of the guests turned to see what was amiss. As I said, I was a bit totty, otherwise I would have been more discreet. Instead, I wiped my sleeve across my mouth to remove his kiss, then I told Lord Durham I should as willingly suffer the fires of hell as let him into my bed."

She laughed then, though the sound held no trace of humor. "I suppose he took me at my word, for that night my bed was set afire."

Eugenia shivered at the horror of such a frightful experience. "What of Durham? Was he not made to pay for his crime?"

Henrietta shook her head. "I could prove nothing. I saw no one in my room, and his lordship had an alibi for the time of the fire. He was at his club, playing whist."

"But he could have hired someone to do his bidding. It is an unfortunate fact that London is filled with felons willing to do any sort of reprehensible act for a few coins."

"Exactly. And once the job is done, those felons can be paid to flee, or they can be got rid of, with no one to care if they are never heard from again."

"So nothing was done?"

"Nothing was done," she replied. "No one doubts that Durham was responsible for the fire and my injuries, but I am—well, I am what I am—and he is a member of the peerage. In such circumstances, justice has a way of turning a blind eye."

Ever empathetic with those who are without power in a sometimes unequal world, Eugenia reached out and took the woman's hands in hers. "I am sorry—for your pain and for the injustice."

Returning the pressure of her hands, Henrietta said,

"Then you will continue with the plan? You will allow me to assist you in taking revenge upon Lord Durham? Though it will not be the full extent of what he deserves, it will be something." She looked into Eugenia's eyes, her own imploring. "You must give me this small share in your own revenge. Please, my dear, say you will not deprive me once again."

Having seen the woman's injuries and heard her story, Eugenia was unable to say her nay. With a sigh of resignation, she said, "Bring in the seamstress."

While Henrietta went to pull the bell to summon the servant, Eugenia asked her if the score Nathan Seymour wished to settle with Lord Durham had to do with the fire.

The woman shook her head. "I am not privy to his reasons. And even if I knew them, I would not betray his trust. If you wish to know Nathan's story, you will be obliged to ask him yourself."

Chapter Five

"If you wish to know Nathan's story, you will be obliged to ask him yourself." While Eugenia prepared for dinner that evening, those words kept intruding upon her thoughts.

She had spent the remainder of the afternoon with Henrietta Parker, obliged to stand for what seemed like hours while dress after dress was tried on her. The seamstress worked quickly and skillfully, pinning and taking tucks here and there—mostly in the bosom—until the dresses were a perfect fit.

Later, while Eugenia and Henrietta had their tea, the seamstress and the lady's maid took themselves off and plied their needles. By the time Eugenia was ready to return to Grosvenor Square, the maid had brought in two bandboxes and a large hatbox. "This will do you for this evening and tomorrow," Henrietta had said. "The others will be sent along as soon as possible."

Eugenia had thanked all three women, but only when Fiona entered the bedchamber with the freshly pressed dinner dress across her arm was she aware of the magic that had been wrought. The dress was a beautiful cinnamon-colored jaconet, and even before Eugenia slipped the delicate creation over her head, she knew it outshone anything she had even worn before.

"Oh, miss," Fiona said, "it's a fairy princess you are.

Or you will be once you've put on the necklace. 'Ere, let me fasten the garrets for you."

"Garnets," Eugenia corrected. She placed the jewelry—a row of lovely teardrop stones—around her neck, then bent down so the child could reach the clasp.

Fiona's mouth was agape. "Oh, miss."

Barely less impressed herself, Eugenia stared at the person in the looking glass, unable to believe what she saw. Henrietta had given her a pot of lip salve and one of powder, but both containers remained as yet unopened upon the dresser. She had, however, taken the woman's advice about arranging her wavy hair loosely, using combs to hold it gently on either side and allowing a spray of curls to fall free of the topknot. It was a simple style, yet it made what Eugenia had always considered a long neck appear graceful and rather swanlike.

If the high waist of the dress was a bit snug, with a tendency to push the wearer's bosom up and out, very nearly causing it to spill over the low neckline in a most revealing manner, Eugenia accepted Henrietta's word that it was the latest style among the *ton*. Stylish or not, Eugenia was grateful to have the borrowed garnets, for the necklace would divert attention from the ample display of flesh.

That naive assumption lasted only as long as it took her to reach the ground-floor drawing room.

To her chagrin, the jewelry did not work nearly so efficiently as she had hoped. When Nathan Seymour turned from the marble mantel to greet her, his gaze went unashamedly to that display of feminine charms—went there and lingered for several seconds. While warmth stole up Eugenia's neck, Nathan slowly transferred his attention to her face.

"Madam," he said, one eyebrow raised in a sardonic manner, almost as if he acknowledged a joke played upon himself, "you find me speechless."

Not certain what the remark signified, and remembering their conversation the day she first came to this house, she said, "Have you words enough to tell me if I have crossed that subtle line?"

His puzzled expression said he did not understand the question. "You once asked me, sir, if I was prepared to cross that subtle line between attracting a man's attention and displaying a sort of blatant voluptuousness."

"Ah, yes." Nathan recalled the discussion now, though there was certainly nothing blatant about the woman who stood before him. The little brown dunnock might be clothed in peacock's feathers, but she had not shed her true nature. Her reserve—her innocence— showed through, and had she but known it, those qualities only added to her appeal.

A moment ago, when he first beheld her, she had, indeed, left him speechless. Here was a woman who would attract any man's attention. The night before, when she had dined with him and Winny, she had been unexpectedly pretty, but now she was positively breathtaking.

"Are you saying, 'Yes,' you remember the conversation?" she asked, the concern in her voice bringing his thoughts back to the present, "or, 'Yes,' I have crossed the line?"

"No, no. Not a bit of it, madam. My affirmative reply was for the former, I assure you."

He stepped forward, took her hand, and lifted it above her head, turning her slowly, as if she danced the minuet. After looking her over, he said, "My congratulations, Eugenia. You look very nice. And quite tonish."

At his words, she blushed, giving the lie to the sophisticated new image, and without thinking, he touched his finger to one pink-hued cheek. Her skin was warm and unbelievably soft. "If you are to play this part successfully, Eugenia, you must learn to accept compliments. You are a woman, full grown. Are you so unaccustomed to being looked over by a man?"

For just a moment, the pink intensified, then her chin lifted rather determinedly. "I am accustomed to being overlooked, sir. As for being looked over, that may take some getting used to."

Though her tone all but dared him to show the least sympathy for her, there was in her dark eyes a look of vulnerability that made him long, just for the moment, to take her in his arms and assure her that she was beautiful. Wisdom prevailed, however, and he released her hand and stepped back.

"Practice is what you need, madam, and since you are dressed for the part, perhaps now is as good a time as any for you to assume the role of my supposed inamorata. What say you? Shall we begin the lessons?"

She seemed to relax. "By all means. If there is one thing I am familiar with, it is lessons."

"Then let us see if you are as good a student as you are an instructress. First," he said, "you must avoid coarse overtures. Though some men find such action pleasing, I am not among their number. I would never have such a woman under my protection, and Lord Durham knows it."

"The subtle line," she reiterated.

"Exactly. From time to time, however, you will want to demonstrate suitable, yet discreet, signs of affection toward me. A momentary touch should do the trick."

"A discreet touch. Yes, I can do that."

"Naturally, I will respond to each of your gestures with appropriate, if slightly less circumspect, exhibitions of proprietorship."

The look she gave him held a hint of suspicion, and more than a trace of obstinacy. "Proprietorship?"

" 'Tis but a word, madam. One a ladybird would not find offensive. Do not be alarmed, for I shall do nothing more overt than slip an arm around your waist or whisper a private word in your ear. You need have no fear that I will forget ours is only a make-believe liaison."

"I . . . I never supposed you would forget it."

Having been accustomed most of his adult life to females who welcomed his attentions, Nathan found her defensiveness annoying. Wishing he had never agreed to this farce, he suggested rather abruptly, "If you cannot bring yourself to touch me, or have me touch you, just do that thing you women do with your eyes."

She stared at him as if she had not the least idea to what he referred.

"Spare me an enactment of coyness, madam. You must know the thing I mean, for all you females resort to it when you wish to get a man's attention. Every female, from green girl to courtesan, employs the technique."

"As it happens," she said, her voice so cool one might be forgiven for thinking *he* had angered *her*, "I am neither a green girl nor a courtesan, and I do not know what you mean."

From the seriousness of her countenance, Nathan was obliged to accept that she was in earnest. He had always assumed that women were born knowing the basics of flirtation. Obviously, it was not so. "Did your mother never teach you to—"

"My mother died when I was eleven years old," she said quietly. "Our time together was too short, and far too precious for anything but the essential lessons."

Nathan bit back an oath. He had forgotten that she was orphaned early. "Forgive me," he said. "I am not usually so maladroit."

"Not at all," she replied softly. "You could not know."

Her graciousness prompted him to make a peace offering by asking the nature of those lessons. Though he expected her reply to include the usual female studies—

needlework, a bit of painting, perhaps a little house-wifery—he soon discovered his error.

"Surely the essentials do not change," she said, apparently surprised by the question. "Be true to yourself, Be fair. Treat others as you would wish to be treated. And most of all, strive to do at least one deed that leaves this Earth a little better for your having lived upon it."

He must have looked as surprised as he felt, for she said, "Are these lessons so different from those your mother taught you?"

No one who knew his thrice-married mother, the new Lady Wrexton, would have asked such a question, and the unexpectedness of it caused Nathan to speak before he thought. "My mother's notion of essentials includes wealth, prestige, and social position, in that order. As for teaching those principles to me, she was always far too busy pursuing her goals to devote much time to me or to my education. For this, I suppose I should be thankful."

The words had only just left his mouth when Nathan wished he could take them back. Without meaning to, or knowing why, he had revealed more of himself to this woman than he had ever revealed to another living soul. Now, of course, it was he who felt vulnerable. Since it was not a feeling he liked, he returned rather hastily to the subject of what women do with their eyes. "It is quite simple," he began, staring at a spot just above her head. "The woman looks at the man, allowing her gaze to linger upon him until he notices her."

"Like this?" she asked.

He was obliged to turn his attention to her, he could do nothing else, and when he looked down at her, he discovered her lovely eyes raised to his. There was within those warm brown depths a gentleness he had never seen before—a sort of fellow-feeling that made him want to reach out and touch her.

He put his hands behind his back, locking the fingers together. "Very good," he said, trying to keep his tone instructional. "Very good, indeed."

"What does the woman do next?" she asked, still gazing into his eyes.

"Next?" He cleared his throat. "Once the man returns the woman's look, she looks away, her eyes downcast."

She did as he instructed, slowly lowering her eyelids until he could see nothing but the reddish-brown lashes that rested upon the satiny smoothness of her cheekbones. Her action had been without guile, yet his lips itched to lean forward and press a kiss upon her cheekbone, to see for himself if the lashes were as downy soft as they appeared.

"Is there more?" she asked, finally looking up at him again.

He nodded. "You may wish to stand just that extra step closer than may be altogether comfortable, and when you do . . ."

"Like this?" she asked, moving to within inches of him.

"Something like that," he replied, trying to ignore the sudden rush of energy surging through his body.

"Shall I touch you now?" she asked, her hand moving slowly toward his forearm.

It was as well for the future of their scheme against Lord Durham that Riddle chose that moment to scratch at the door, for Nathan was not certain what he would have answered to Eugenia's question about touching him. Wisdom told him he should say her nay, but the man in him wanted to bid her touch him immediately.

"Enter," he called, taking a step back before the door swung open.

"If it please you, sir," the butler said, "dinner is served."

*   *   *

Their dinner was far more agreeable than Eugenia had anticipated, especially considering those few minutes in the drawing room—minutes in which she had discovered a vulnerability in Nathan Seymour and a susceptibility in herself. She had feared the meal would be awkward, but nothing could have been further from the truth, for when Nathan set himself to please, he was charming enough to make any woman feel as though she were the most interesting person in the world.

Not that *she* believed it for a moment.

Surely it was a technique of some sort—something men of the world did instinctively in much the same way the kind of women Nathan knew flirted with their eyes. He probably treated every woman of his acquaintance in just that same manner: asking her questions, listening to the answers, even laughing when she made a small jest.

As for the way he had watched her while she spoke, with his attention riveted upon her face, and the way a flash of liveliness had shown in his blue-gray eyes just seconds before his lips broke into a smile, surely those actions meant nothing. A woman would be a fool to assign them the least importance—especially a woman like her, a woman who was out of her sphere.

At the remembered word, Eugenia sensibly came back down to earth. Nathan Seymour was merely being a good host, much as Mr. Winfield had been the evening before; no point in giving it more significance than it merited.

She recalled that Henrietta Parker had dropped a hint or two this morning about Nathan's habit of never remaining involved with a mistress or a flirt for more than a few weeks. "He always tells them ahead of time how it will be," Henrietta had said. "He does not want a lengthy relationship, and any female who aligns herself with him would be wise to believe his warning. Of course, there are always a few who think they can charm him into falling in love with them. Some have even aspired to becoming his wife. Unfortunately, those women deluded themselves, and they paid for the delusion with broken hearts."

She had caught Eugenia's hand to be certain she had her full attention. "My dear, heed my advice: There are no exceptions to the rule. Do not fall in love with Nathan Seymour."

Naturally, Eugenia had informed the woman in no uncertain terms that she had no thought of trying to catch Nathan Seymour. And she meant every word. Being a sensible female, she would not expose herself to certain heartache. If Nathan had been able to withstand the blandishments of some of the loveliest women of the *ton*, he was certainly safe from entrapment by a female with no fortune, no connections, and no pretensions to beauty.

Having reminded herself of her status in the scheme of things, Eugenia renewed her commitment to playing cards with Lord Durham and winning back her cousin's ten thousand pounds. She had no other agenda. She expected no other results.

Once the meal was finished, Nathan chose to forgo the ritual glass of port in favor of accompanying her to the drawing room. She had tried to decline further time spent in his company, giving as her excuse a fatiguing day and a wish to go directly to her bedchamber, but he had said the night was still young.

"If you can delay your rest for another half hour, madam, we should continue the lesson we started earlier, especially if I am to take you driving in the park tomorrow."

"I did not realize we were to begin the charade so soon."

"Why delay? Unless Henrietta was unable to supply you with an appropriate frock."

"She and her women were wonderful, and if you believe Lord Durham will be in the park tomorrow, I will be ready whenever you say."

"I cannot vouch for Durham's movements."

"But if he is not there, what is the point in our going?"

"The point is that others will see us. Or more important, they will see you. The gossips being what they are, I promise you, before nightfall Durham will know of the existence of my beautiful new mistress."

Eugenia felt her breath catch in her throat. Did he really find her beautiful?

No, I will not think of that! I will not delude myself. Never mind the way he had looked at her when he spoke, his blue-gray gaze so intent it made her pulse race.

He looked at her still, the way a man looks at a woman, and she felt an undercurrent of excitement; a hope that anything might be possible. *No! It was part of the lesson, nothing more.*

She breathed deeply, filling her lungs in the hope that the familiarity of the act would help her remain calm. "You are not being very subtle, sir."

His eyebrow lifted as if he was puzzled by her remark. "I beg your pardon?"

"If the way you are looking at me is anything to go by, sir, you seem to have forgotten your own words. Am I expected to respond to such—how did you phrase it— blatant voluptuousness?"

A teasing light shone in his eyes. "A man can only hope, madam."

What was he doing? Eugenia felt off balance, as though she needed to hold on to something for support. "Sir, are you making sport of me?"

"Not at all. If I remember correctly, you said *you* were not prepared to go so far as a quick tumble in the hay. As for me," he continued, his smile causing a frisson of excitement to tingle its way up her spine, "*I* find nothing to dislike about the possibility."

Chapter Six

His words kept her awake half the night, until she finally convinced herself that he had been teasing her. A quick tumble in the hay was the last thing Nathan Seymour wanted. Eugenia had not been deceived. She was no lightskirt, and he had no wish to be caught in parson's mousetrap; otherwise, Fiona would not still be sleeping upon a pallet in the guest bedchamber.

Eugenia and Nathan had agreed to a business arrangement, and once Cedric Durham was separated from his money, the two of them would part ways, never to see one another again. That was Nathan's goal as well as hers. Unfortunately, their first lesson last evening had not gone well. It had become too intense. That was why Nathan had teased her about a tumble in the hay; it was to lighten the tension between them.

She hoped he had found the lesson successful. She certainly had not. If anything, those few minutes had made her more aware of him than ever—aware of his handsome countenance, his charm, and especially aware of that indefinable maleness that made so many women fall under his spell. Refusing to be among their number, Eugenia had told him she was too tired to remain belowstairs another minute, and after a quick curtsy, she bid him good night and rushed from the room. Only after she reached the safety of her bedchamber did her heart cease its mad pounding against her chest.

Now it was time to join him for their drive in the park. Thankfully, the harsh realities of daylight had brought a return of her sanity, and she felt equal to whatever task was required of her. With a renewed focus on her objective, which was to catch Lord Durham's attention, she donned the rather flashy Prussian blue carriage dress with its double row of flounces at the hem, then topped it off with a darker blue spencer and a matching silk bonnet.

Remembering her wish not to be recognized after this escapade was finished, Eugenia had asked the seamstress to attach a veil to the bonnet. The good woman's idea of a veil was a totally transparent bit of lace that only just touched the bridge of the wearer's nose, but at a distance it might provide just a hint of concealment. This time Eugenia made use of the pot of lip salve, darkening her lips to a soft berry red, then adding a tiny heart-shaped patch just to the right of her mouth. She felt certain the lace veil and the paint were enough to fool any but the closest of acquaintances, and since she had not the least fear of meeting anyone she knew well, Eugenia descended the stairs with a certain degree of confidence.

That confidence grew when she reached the ground floor and all but bumped into Nathan coming from the drawing room. For a moment he could only stare.

"Upon my word, madam, you shall have all the heads turning in the park." He took her gloved hand and lifted the fingers to his lips. "I only hope I shall not be obliged to use my whip to beat off the gentlemen wishing to make your acquaintance."

Eugenia knew this was but his way of making her feel more relaxed, but she smiled her appreciation nonetheless.

"And if you smile like that at any of the lads," he said,

"I shall probably find myself in a duel come Monday morning."

When she chuckled, he took her hand and placed it in the crook of his arm, leading her toward the wide oak entrance door. "Am I to understand from your apparent amusement, madam, that you do not find my compliments offensive? I had it on good authority that ladies did not appreciate such flattery."

"Ladies do not, sir. Once we walk out that door, however, I am no longer a lady. I am a lady*bird*."

He was still laughing when they reached the pavement, where the curricle waited.

They said nothing more until he helped her up into the leather seat, climbed up beside her, then bid the groom stand away from the chestnuts' heads.

They traveled upper Grosvenor Street to Park Lane, then entered Hyde Park at the south gate. The carriage drive was a broad avenue with tall, thick walnut trees on the east side, their wide-spreading crowns offering shade on the sunny June day, and on the west side lovely beds of white columbine and pink and purple petunias.

Vehicles of every description filled the carriage drive—from landaus conveying sedate matrons and their pretty charges to high-perch phaetons driven by young gentlemen sporting outlandishly high collars and brightly colored waistcoats—and from Rotten Row to their right came the sound of the myriad hoofbeats of the saddle horses.

"We chose a fine day for our drive," Nathan offered as an opening gambit. "Everyone and his wife seems to be abroad."

"Are they all wives?" she asked. "Am I the only ladybird?"

"Not at all. Over there," he said, looking toward a yellow-trimmed whiskey pulled by a showy roan. The driver was a female with hair as improbably yellow as the vehicle she drove, and every few yards she slowed traffic to a crawl by waving to some young buck who tipped his hat in greeting then stopped for a word.

Remembering that she was supposed to attract attention as well, Eugenia took advantage of the momentary pause in traffic to single out a lone gentleman in a phaeton, a portly man no longer in his youth. Recalling her lesson of the evening before, she lifted the lace veil and gazed at the man from the corner of her eye, continuing until he glanced in her direction. She forced herself not to look away until she was quite certain he knew she was looking at him, then she lowered her lashes.

As though she were a magnet and he a piece of metal, the fellow was beside their curricle within seconds, his curly brim beaver lifted from his slightly balding head.

"Seymour," the gentleman greeted, his eyes all but bulging as a result of his too-tight waistcoat, "ain't seen you around lately."

"No," Nathan answered, his tone sarcastic, "not since Midsummer's Eve. What was that, all of two days ago?"

If Eugenia considered this reply rather rude, the gentleman seemed not to notice. If the truth be told, he was paying very little attention to Nathan; he was far too interested in ogling her. Though it was why they had come to the park, Eugenia found such open admiration almost more than she could endure.

"I say, Seymour, what does a fellow have to do to get an introduction to this fair vision?"

Aware that no gentleman would speak thus in front of a lady, Eugenia felt her cheeks grow warm.

"Strap me," the fellow said, "she blushes!" Giving Nathan a broad wink, he said, "Damn your eyes, Seymour, how do you always manage to get them fresh off the farm? Mark my words, they'll be entering bets in the book to see who succeeds you."

Eugenia was not certain to what he referred, but she

felt Nathan stiffen beside her. At that moment the traffic began to move again, so he nodded to the plump gentleman and gave the horses the notice to move on.

If the gentleman thought this rude behavior, he said nothing, merely tipped his hat and bid them both farewell. "Until we meet again, Fair Vision."

They had gone scarce fifteen yards when they were approached by another gentleman, this one much younger than the last, and far more subtle.

"Seymour," he began, doffing his hat, "been meaning to look you up."

"Have you now? To what purpose?"

"Cannot recall at the moment," he replied, smiling at Eugenia, "but give me a few minutes and I feel certain it will come to me."

Taking the initiative, Eugenia said, "How vexatious to forget a thing. Perhaps you should put a string around your finger, sir."

The gentleman made her a partial bow. "Just the thing, ma'am. You are kind to suggest it." He turned to Nathan then, a look of anticipation in his eyes, but when no introduction was forthcoming, he bowed again. "Alvin Comstock, ma'am, at your service. Is this your first visit to town? I know you cannot have been here long, else every fellow within fifty miles would have been talking about it."

Eugenia lowered her lashes, and when she looked at him again, she smiled. "I am newly come to town, Mr. Comstock."

"By Jove," he said, encouraged by her response, "if I may be so bold, ma'am, might I be allowed to show you a few of the sights?"

"Give over, Comstock," a tall, dark-haired gentleman said, attempting to bring his stanhope close to the curricle. "You are blocking traffic."

"Stubble it, Wilson, I saw her first. Besides, Seymour

is acting like a monk held by a vow of silence, and I have not even learned the beauty's name."

Eugenia discovered a most unladylike desire to laugh, for if these two had met her a week ago, they would not have so much as raised an eyebrow. "La, sir," she said, "what do names matter?"

"Upon my word, ma'am, that is an excellent question. It is like the poet says, 'A rose by any other name,' don't you know."

Though Eugenia was familiar with the reference, she tried for a puzzled expression. "But my name is not Rose, sir. I assure you."

Her two auditors laughed as though charmed, though Nathan remained silent. At that moment traffic began to move again, but before Nathan could encourage the horses, another gentleman stopped, effectively putting an end to their progress. "I say, Nate, old boy."

Mr. Martin Winfield tipped his hat to Eugenia. "Well met, ma'am. How do you do?"

"I am well, thank you, Winny."

"Ho!" Mr. Comstock said, glancing at Mr. Winfield, "are you acquainted with this beauty in blue?"

"I am acquainted enough to have procured the first waltz at White's ball," he replied, "but more I will not say."

The tall gentleman and Mr. Comstock spoke at once. "May I have the honor of partnering you as well, ma'am?"

Eugenia looked at Nathan, as if for consent, then she turned her attention back to her admirers. "I should be delighted, sirs."

"Kindly move on!" called a white-haired gentleman in the carriage just behind them. Since he escorted two very starched-up matrons, both of whom held their noses in the air as though they had caught the aroma of bad fish, the gathering of gentlemen dispersed, allowing Nathan to move his curricle out of the way.

Nathan and Eugenia remained in the park only as long as it took them to reach the nearest gate, but at every turn they were stopped by lone gentlemen wanting an introduction to Nathan's newest conquest. No one was so rewarded, and by the time the curricle and pair finally exited the park and traveled back up Park Lane to Upper Grosvenor, Eugenia sensed that Nathan was angry. Though why he should be so, she could not even imagine. She had certainly played her part just as he had told her.

"What has put you out of sorts?" she asked.

"Nothing," he answered, his voice cold.

"Then what is amiss? Have I said or done something?"

He muttered an oath beneath his breath. "Why must females always conclude that everything has to do with them?"

"And why," she countered, "must males always assume they have the right to vent their ill temper on whoever is unfortunate enough to be close at hand?"

Nathan was taken aback, both by her outspokenness and by the unanswerable truthfulness of her observation. He *was* angry, and it had *everything* to do with her. But he could not tell her that. How could he explain that he had wanted to put his fist through more than one leering face in the park? Or that he had not liked the familiar way that loose fish, Alvin Comstock, had ogled her. Never mind that she was dressed as a lightskirt; she was, in fact, a lady, and she deserved to be treated as a lady.

"Are you annoyed because Lord Durham was not in the park?"

"No. As I told you before, he will hear of your existence. By this evening, that scoundrel, Comstock, will be boasting to anyone who will listen that he charmed the unknown Cyprian in blue into granting him a dance at the masquerade ball."

She raised her brows, for all the world as though she was interested. "Is he a scoundrel?" she asked, apparently willing to ignore the fact that her existence, if not her name, would be the latest *on dit* in the gentlemen's clubs. "I rather liked him."

Women! There was no understanding them.

"I realize," she continued, "that he is not nearly so dastardly as Lord Durham, nor yet such a devilish fellow with the ladies as you are reputed to be. However, since he was a genuine admirer, and I have not had so many of those in my life, I am inclined to think him a very pretty-behaved fellow. Furthermore—"

"Who said I was a devilish fellow with the ladies?"

She placed her forefinger to her chin as if giving the matter thought. "I cannot vouch for who first said it, but I believe it is common knowledge."

It was as well that Nathan saw her lips twitch, for his annoyance vanished immediately. "I trust you will let me know, madam, when you are quite finished making a May game of me."

She laughed then, and a rather saucy look shone in her brown eyes. "I could not resist, sir. My father used to say that my mother was a bit of an imp. I suppose I inherited it from her. Will you forgive me?"

With Eugenia smiling up at him, her mouth relaxed, Nathan had little trouble forgiving her. In fact, he was tempted to see if those painted lips tasted anything like the berries that supposedly stained them.

Fortunately, she had no notion what he wished to do, and after schooling her face, she said, "You have my promise, sir, henceforth I will be very serious. Especially at the masked ball."

Happy to have something other than her lips to occupy his thoughts, he said, "By the way, can you dance?"

Those brown eyes lit up again. "If you are worried that I will disgrace you, sir, there is but one way to know for certain."

Her challenge seemed to hang in the air, and while Nathan was lost in thought considering the possibility of dancing with her, and perhaps holding her in his arms, they arrived at the town house. Thankfully, the necessity for controlling the horses gave him a moment in which to bring his wayward thoughts under control as well.

He reined in the chestnuts, and while still holding the ribbons firmly between his fingers, he offered Eugenia a hand down to the pavement. As soon as she was on firm ground, he lifted his hat and bid her a pleasant afternoon, informing her that he had something to attend to at his club. "I doubt I shall see you again until tomorrow."

Unable to stop herself, Eugenia asked, "But what of our lessons? The ball is but six days hence. What if I am not ready?"

"You will be."

"But I . . . I do not know how to waltz."

"What?"

"Winny has claimed the first waltz, and though I know the country dances, I have never learned to—"

"Damnation," he muttered not quite far enough beneath his breath for her to avoid overhearing, "it wanted only that."

His voice sounded odd, and Eugenia began to wonder if he might be heartily sick of trying to teach her. Was she so impossible?

Pride came to her rescue, stiffening her shoulders and firming her chin. "If you find the idea so unpalatable, sir, you need not teach me to dance. I shall merely explain to Mr. Winfield that I cannot waltz. I am persuaded he will understand. As for the continuation of my lessons," she added, her voice filled with resolve, "you promised to teach me how to attract Lord Durham's attention, and I mean to hold you to your word. Time is running out, and I am not yet ready to face that particular scoundrel."

To her surprise, Nathan shook his head. "I am beginning to think, Eugenia, that you know more than I gave you credit for knowing. There is such a thing as native ability."

With that she was obliged to be satisfied, for he tipped his hat and urged the horses forward. She stood and watched him until the curricle disappeared around the corner, then she climbed the three stone steps to the wide, oak door and lifted the brass knocker and let it fall. The sharp sound echoed inside the building. When no one came to admit her, she was obliged to sound the knocker once again.

Several moments passed before the door swung open. Riddle stepped back to let her enter the vestibule, but he offered no apology for the delay. Instead, his middle-aged face was a study in disapproval.

After Nathan's unexplainable behavior, Eugenia found the butler's rebuff doubly disturbing. It was odd, but she had been untroubled by the knowledge that the gentlemen in Hyde Park thought she was Nathan's mistress. The case was quite otherwise with Nathan's servants. It embarrassed Eugenia that they believed her to be a woman of easy virtue.

Knowing there was nothing she could say to change Riddle's opinion, she merely nodded, then strolled past him, her destination the staircase and ultimately the privacy of her bedchamber. Once again, solitude was denied her, for she found Fiona there, with rags and a pail of soapy water, scrubbing the hearth. At Eugenia's sudden entrance, the child jumped and cried out, spilling water on the blue and silver carpet.

"Oh, miss!" Fiona said, her hand to her thin throat, "you fair gave me a fright. I thought you might be—" She smothered the words and turned back to the hearth to grab a dry cloth. "Excuse the mess, miss. I'll 'ave this done in two shakes, I will."

It did not need a genius to see Fiona was frightened, and not for a moment did Eugenia think the maid was frightened of her. "What is it, Fiona? What has happened?"

The young maid began dabbing at the damp carpet. "It's nofing, miss. Just . . ."

"Just what?" she asked, kneeling down so she was on the child's eye level. "You may tell me."

Fiona looked up for a moment, and in her pale blue eyes Eugenia saw fear—fear quickly denied. "It b'aint nofing, miss. I was wiping the windowsill a minute ago, and I thought I saw someone."

"Who did you think you saw?"

"I thought it was me uncle, but 'appen I was mistaken. What would 'e being doing 'ere in Mayfair?"

Eugenia had thought Fiona was alone in the world, but apparently she was mistaken. She was about to ask the child why she was afraid of her own uncle, when Fiona turned away, her thin shoulders and back effectively demonstrating that she wanted no more questions.

Forced to respect the girl's wishes, Eugenia contented herself with saying she was certain they were all safe here in Mr. Seymour's house. "After all, other than the master, who would not let anyone hurt you, there are also Riddle and the two footmen. I believe we may safely trust in four healthy males to keep the wolves from our door."

" 'Appen you're right, miss. 'Twere foolish of me to act so chicken'earted. I'll worrit no more about it." She uttered an unconvincing laugh, then gave the hearth a final swipe with a dry cloth. "There! Clean and bright. I'll just take this mess away."

With that, she gathered up her pail and rags and hurried from the room, and Eugenia was left to make what she would of the child's behavior. Not that she thought overlong on the subject, for she had concerns of her own, principal of which was the masked ball six days hence, and Nathan Seymour's very peculiar behavior after their ride in the park.

As Nathan had informed her, he was from home that evening, but when he absented himself the next evening and the following one as well, Eugenia began to wonder if she would see him at all before time to dress for the masquerade. And what of Lord Durham? She was not nearly so confident as Nathan that the scoundrel would seek her out at the ball. Why should he? After all, she was not such a beauty that a mere hour's ride in the park would send half the male population in search of her.

By Wednesday afternoon, she decided she had twiddled her thumbs long enough. The ball was but two days away, and if she was to meet Lord Durham, she felt certain she needed to show herself about town at least once more. With that in mind, she bid Fiona tell Riddle she needed the landau in half an hour. "And fetch your wrap. For I will want you to accompany me to Hatchard's. I find I am in need of a good book."

"A book, miss?" The youngster looked incredulous. "You've no need to bestir yourself for a book. The guv 'as got a room full of them. 'Appen you could take your pick."

Since all the logic was on Fiona's side, Eugenia chose not to argue. Instead, she merely smiled and said she wanted a book of her own. With that, the young girl was unable to argue, and she went first to give Riddle the message about the landau, then she went up to her attic room to fetch her things.

While Fiona was gone, Eugenia chose one of the walking dresses Henrietta Parker's seamstress had delivered Saturday afternoon. It was a brassy frock both in its style and in its color, but the dark, metallic chambray quite suited Eugenia's coloring. As for the snug fit of the waist and the far-too-revealing neckline, she was honest enough to admit those features were enough to catch any male's attention.

Over the dress she fastened an elbow-length mantle of transparent lace that was certain to tease the viewer's imagination without adding one whit to the wearer's modesty. After applying a touch of lip salve, and dusting just a thin layer of powder across her nose and cheek-bones, she donned a straw bonnet dyed to match the dress and tied the wide satin ribbons just in front of her left ear. The ornate black feather she positioned so it curled around the right side of her face. Her true identity effectively concealed from all but the most discerning eye, and looking every inch the lightskirt, Eugenia grabbed up the matching reticule and descended the carpeted stairs, where Riddle waited, disapproval writ plainly upon his face.

Without uttering a word, the butler opened the wide oak door, then he closed it with a decided bang almost before Eugenia had reached the bottom step. Trying to ignore the rudeness, she told the driver to take her to Hatchard's, then she climbed into the carriage with Fiona, sitting back as comfortably as possible while they made their way the short distance to number eighty-seven Piccadilly.

She was too nervous about what she planned to do to give much thought to Fiona's quick, furtive glances, and once they climbed from the carriage and entered the celebrated bookshop, with its small-paned bow windows on either side of the entrance, she dismissed the child completely from her mind. "Wait over there," she said, pointing to a small settle at the rear of the shop, where a pair of uniformed maids waited for the young ladies in their charge.

It being too early for the afternoon ride in the park, a dozen or so patrons milled around the shop, some strolling up and down the stacks of books while others sat on conveniently placed benches and conversed with acquaintances. Eugenia glanced around, but saw no one she knew. Once when she made eye contact with a young lady, the damsel's mother pinched the chit's arm and said, "Ignore the creature."

Feeling the heat of embarrassment warm her entire body, Eugenia pretended interest in the first book she put her hand to.

"A very dry tome, ma'am," said a tall, dark-eyed gentleman with a handsome, if rather dissolute-looking face, "unless you have an interest in tisanes and nostrums."

Only then did Eugenia notice the title of the book she held; it was a treatise on seventeenth-century cure-alls by a Doctor Josiah Fenton. Remembering her true purpose for coming to Hatchard's, Eugenia gave a little shudder and shoved the volume back upon the shelf.

"A wise move," the gentleman said, a not unappealing smile showing strong, even teeth. "Allow me to escort you to the next shelf over."

He was older than Nathan Seymour, probably thirty-five or six, and where Nathan was fair and muscular, this man was dark and quite slender, with black, wavy hair and eyes the color of newly mined coal.

After offering her his arm, which she took without a moment's hesitation, he said, "Allow me to introduce myself. I am Durham."

A shudder must have run through Eugenia, for her escort put his hand over hers, where it rested on his forearm. "No need to be afraid of me, my pretty, I mean you no harm."

Bidding herself remember that she was supposed to be accomplished at the art of flirting, she smiled and looked away, feigning interest in the novels on the shelf they were approaching.

"A woman alone," she said, pulling a book from the

shelf, "must always be a bit afraid, my lord. You are a lord, are you not?"

He nodded, the gesture urbane, sophisticated, and she looked up at him with what she hoped was a wide-eyed, innocent gaze. "Not that I care about such things as titles, mind you, for I can tell by your manners that you are a gentleman of distinction."

"And you," he said, bending close to her ear, "are an angel, newly come from heaven."

Eugenia resisted the desire to move away from him, instead taking refuge behind lowered lashes. "Sir," she said, "you should not pay me such pretty compliments."

"Oh? And why should I not?"

She removed her hand from his arm. "Because we are only just met and may never meet again."

"The former may be true, my lovely, but I assure you, the latter is not." He caught her hand and lifted it to his lips. "I mean to know you much better, beginning with your name."

Eugenia eased her hand from his. Though she wanted nothing so much as to wipe her hand down the side of her skirt to remove the imprint of his kiss, she refrained from doing so. Instead, she smiled to show she was not offended by anything he had said or done.

Having achieved the purpose for which she had come—to meet Lord Durham—she wanted to exit quickly. "I must go," she said, "for I am to drive in the park within the hour."

"But you cannot leave," he said. "You have not told me your name."

"Did I not?" she said, somehow manufacturing a brief chuckle. "How remiss of me." With that, she handed him the novel she held and turned away, signaling to Fiona to join her. Within moments they were outside the bookshop, hurrying down the street.

"Where we 'eaded, miss?"

"Anyplace," Eugenia replied, "just as long as it is away from here."

The youngster pointed to a spot across the street. "That be the guv's landau, miss. You want I should go tell the groom to come fetch you?"

Eugenia looked where the child pointed. Recognizing the driver, she breathed a sigh of relief. "We will both go," she said, then grabbed Fiona's hand, and the two of them hurried across to the waiting carriage.

Still trembling from her encounter with Lord Durham, Eugenia had never been so glad of anything as she was to arrive back in Grosvenor Square. As soon as the carriage stopped, she alit and climbed the stairs, leaving Fiona to tell the groom they would not need him again.

To Eugenia's relief, Riddle chose not to take his time about admitting her, instead opening the door promptly. Since he wore the contemptuous expression that was his usual manner when forced to serve her, she did not bother to greet him, but went directly to the staircase. At that moment, she wanted nothing so much as to reach her room, where she might bring some order to her disordered senses. She had just placed her hand upon the polished newel post when she heard the sound of hurried footfalls, as though someone ran up the stone steps.

Eugenia turned in time to see the unwary Riddle, who was in the act of closing the door, knocked aside as Fiona pushed with all her might against the heavy oak. Eugenia was hardly less surprised than the butler when the child cried, " 'Elp me!"

Running straight for Eugenia, Fiona fell on her knees in supplication. "It's 'im," she said. " 'E's glimmed me, 'e 'as, and now 'e'll be wanting to take me back to that place. I don't want to go there."

The child began to sob. "Don't let 'im take me, miss.

They'll make me do them shameful things, and I'll surely die of the pox, same as Ada, and go straight to 'ell."

Eugenia had no difficulty in piecing together the child's story. Miss Eugenia Bailey might be a gentleman's daughter, supposedly sheltered from the seamier aspects of life, but she knew the significance of the pox, and she could easily guess at the type of place where a female—even one who was still a child—would be made to commit shameful acts.

She caught Fiona by the shoulders and urged her to her feet. "You are safe, child. Have no fear, this man, whoever he may be, will not harm you."

" 'E's me uncle, or so 'e says, and 'e'll be wanting to take me back to that place, else they'll not pay 'im. And next time they'll dope me, or put me in a room without a window so's I can't climb—"

She got no further, for two sets of boots now sounded on the stone stairs.

"Riddle!" Eugenia ordered, "close the door! Quickly!"

The butler had been so surprised by the skinny little maid's hasty entrance—and through the front door, of all places!—that he had stood motionless, his mouth agape, while she told her disjointed story. Now, as he tried to obey Eugenia's order, he found himself pushed aside once again, the door all but torn from his hands.

"That's 'er!" shouted a tall, thin fellow dressed in a laborer's smock, stained twill trousers, and a billed cap. "That's me niece," he said to the grizzled little man who accompanied him—a chimney sweep if the ground-in smut on his face and hands was anything to go by. " 'Elp me catch 'er, for she's slippery as a bleedin' eel."

Eugenia pushed Fiona behind her. "What is the meaning of this?" she demanded of the intruders, her tone as regal as that of a duchess, and twice as affronted. "How dare you force your way into a gentleman's establishment."

The grizzled little man stopped just inside the doorway, but the tall fellow in the cap came all the way into the vestibule, looking about him suspiciously. He pointed his finger at Fiona, who hid behind Eugenia. "Me name's Jem Weems," he said, "and that's me niece, Fiona, what run away. I've come to take 'er back, and I b'aint leaving 'ere without 'er."

Fiona buried her face in Eugenia's back, her thin, trembling body pressed against that of the woman who was her only hope of deliverance. Feeling the child's terror, Eugenia knew she could not let this lout so much as lay a hand on the little girl. "Riddle," she said, assuming her duchess voice again, "fetch the footmen, and have these persons thrown from the premises."

Riddle tried to do her bidding, but Weems stopped him by pressing his dirty hand into the butler's chest and shoving him back against the wall. "Stay where you are, Prune Face, else you'll be the sorrier for it."

With a sense of impending doom, Eugenia watched the man put his hand inside his smock and remove a crudely fashioned, but nonetheless lethal-looking knife. "And now," he said, turning back to Eugenia, "gimme that brat."

In no doubt of the man's ability to use the weapon, Eugenia knew nothing else to do but continue her bluff. "How dare you speak to me in that manner, you lout. When my husband, the Duke of Bailey, hears of this outrage, he will contact Bow Street and have you arrested. I suggest you leave now if you wish to avoid being transported."

The grizzled fellow tugged at the smock. "C'mon, Jem. Let's get out of 'ere. That scrawny little gal won't fetch enough to make it wurf our while, and I want no dealings with dukes what'll take it into their 'ead to see a man transported."

"Lummox," Weems said, "she ain't no duke's missus."

He looked her up and down. "Use your glimmers, fool. Can't you see she's painted up like one of them fancy pieces?"

Weems took a step toward Eugenia, the knife raised menacingly. "Now, gimme."

More frightened than she had ever been in her life, Eugenia began inching her way toward the cherry console table, her hope to grab one of the candlesticks as a weapon to defend herself. She was still several feet from her objective when help came from an unexpected source.

"Her Grace is telling the truth," Riddle said. "The duke should be returning any minute. He is most attached to the duchess, and if any harm should befall her, I assure you His Grace will not rest until he sees the two of you chained to a ship bound for Australia."

While her heart threatened to pound its way right out of her chest, Eugenia watched Weems measure the butler's words against the evidence of his own eyes. He looked her over once again, and though he snarled like some feral animal, he began to back toward the entrance. His abetter needed no encouragement to turn and flee down the steps, and within a matter of seconds, Weems turned and followed suit.

Spurred to action, Riddle lost no time in shutting the door, and only after he had shot home the iron bolt did he allow himself the luxury of slumping against the solid oak panels.

"Come here," Eugenia said, pulling Fiona from behind her and enfolding the shivering child in her arms. "All is well, little one. You need worry no more. I doubt your uncle will have the nerve to return." If her voice trembled as though she had an ague, no one seemed to notice.

While the youngster clung to Eugenia, crying softly, Riddle seemed to regain his strength. Walking purposefully toward the drawing room, he stepped inside and gave several impatient yanks to the cord that rang a bell in the kitchen. Within seconds, one of the footmen arrived on the run.

"Yes, sir, Mr. Riddle."

The butler straightened his shoulders, as if donning his lost dignity, then pointed toward Fiona. "Take the girl to Mrs. Drockett," he ordered, "and see she is given a draft to calm her, for she has had a fright."

"Yes, sir," the servant replied, his eyes wide with surprise.

Suddenly tired beyond belief, Eugenia gave the young girl into the footman's keeping, then turned once again toward the stairs. Her foot had only just touched the first step when Riddle spoke again.

"And, Charles," he said.

"Yes, sir?"

"As soon as Fiona is seen to, have Mrs. Drockett prepare a pot of tea for Miss Eugenia. And tell her I said to see if there are any of those little cinnamon cakes miss liked the other day."

If the footman was surprised by this unexpected show of consideration, Eugenia was flabbergasted. She looked at the butler, who made her a very respectful bow. "The moment the tea is ready, Miss Eugenia, I will have it brought to your chamber."

"Th . . . thank you, Riddle."

"My pleasure, miss."

Chapter Seven

Eugenia did not see Nathan that night, though she knew he had returned home, for the following day Fiona was bundled into the landau and sent to Swanleigh Hall in Hertfordshire. Before she left, however, the youngster had told Eugenia about her escape from the brothel where the man who called himself her uncle had sold her for five pounds.

"I was climbing out the window," she said, "when I 'eard somefing, or someone walking past the alley. I was that frighten, miss, so I tried to climb back up. 'Appen me dress got caught on somefing, and I couldn't go up nor down."

Eugenia muttered a most unladylike oath, furious that a child should have been forced into such a frightening position.

" 'Twere all right, though, miss, for the someone what 'appened by was the guv."

"Mr. Seymour?"

Fiona nodded. " 'E seemed to know what I was doing and why, so 'e tells me to just let go and fall, that 'e'd catch me."

"Oh, no," Eugenia said, frightened for the child even in retrospect.

"Not to worry, miss." Her grin was so big it all but

covered her thin-cheeked face. "The guv, 'e caught me all right."

"Even so, you were very brave."

" 'Twere the guv what was brave, for two very mean bruisers kept order inside that awful place. And strong as 'e is, I misdoubt 'e'd of stood a chance against them two sloggers."

Even after the fact, the thought of what might have happened made Eugenia's stomach queasy. "As you say, Mr. Seymour was quite brave. What happened after he caught you?"

" 'E sets me on me feet, grabs 'old of me 'and, and commences to run, tugging me along behind 'im so fast me feet scarce touched the ground. Only when we were a goodly way from that place did 'e stop so's I could catch me breath, and to make sure b'aint nobody chasing us."

"And were they?"

"Not a soul, miss. We'd got away clean." Her smile vanished. " 'Course, I didn't 'ave no place to go."

Eugenia remembered from an earlier conversation that the youngster had been in the workhouse before coming to work for Nathan.

"When the guv asked me did I want 'im to take me 'ome to me mam and pap, I told 'im I didn't 'ave no mam nor no pap, and I didn't 'ave no 'ome neither. And I told him straight out I didn't want to be took back to the workhouse! After that 'e asks me do I want to work in 'is 'ouse."

It was Eugenia's turn to smile. "And you accepted his offer."

"Coo ee! Didn't I just. The guv brought me 'ere straightaway, and that's when 'e told Mr. Riddle I was to be treated fair and not worked too 'ard, and fed 'til I couldn't eat no more."

When the child gazed pointedly at the currant bun

Eugenia had left on her breakfast tray, Eugenia laughed and told her she would probably end her days as big as Farmer Brown's cow.

"I'd not mind it," Fiona said, snatching the bun and hurrying to the door, "for I'm that fond of milk."

Eugenia was still laughing when someone scratched at her door. Thinking it must be Fiona, returning for the tray, she called permission to enter. To her surprise the person seeking entrance was none other than Creel, Nathan's very proper manservant.

After bowing very politely, the valet said, "Begging your pardon, Miss Eugenia, but Mr. Seymour sends his compliments and asks if you would be so good as to join him for dinner this evening."

Still annoyed that Nathan had kept his distance for almost the entire week, Eugenia was tempted to decline the invitation. Wisdom prevailed, however, and she told the valet to inform his employer that she would be delighted to join him.

She dressed very carefully that evening, in spite of the awkward assistance lent her by Mary, the chambermaid hired that day to take Fiona's place. Her face free of paint and powder, she chose to wear her own gold sarcenet in lieu of one of the more provocative dinner dresses altered for her by Henrietta Parker's seamstress. With her toilette completed, Eugenia made her way down to the drawing room, where a smiling footman announced her as though she were one of a hundred guests.

"So," Nathan said as soon as the footman closed the door, "you have made the acquaintance of Lord Durham."

Taken off guard by this abrupt greeting, she stopped in the middle of the room and stared at Nathan. He stood several feet away, before the niche containing the statue of Urania, almost as if he had been studying the Muse's marble profile. "How did you know I had met him?" she asked.

He returned her look with one that said she had asked a foolish question. "The gossips got wind of that particular piece of news almost before you left Hatchard's."

"Oh."

"Oh, indeed," he said, crossing to within a foot of where she stood, and glaring at her as if she were a headstrong child. "Did I not tell you how it would be? Why could you not trust me to know how to do the thing properly?"

"I am sorry," she said, the coolness of her tone repudiating the words, "but I am not accustomed to trusting my fate to others. How was I to know you had not completely washed your hands of me and my plan? When you all but disappeared, leaving me alone for six days, with no one to advise me upon the subject, I took it upon myself to go to Hatchard's, where I might practice my one and only lesson. My encounter with Lord Durham himself was but a stroke of good fortune."

"Good fortune? You may well have ruined the entire plan!"

Eugenia stiffened. "I do not see that, sir. I do not see that at all. Our meeting lasted no more than a matter of minutes, and in that time I said very little, leaving most of the conversation to Lord Durham. And, before you anger me further, allow me to inform you that my behavior was neither blatant nor voluptuous!"

"*I* anger *you*?"

"Exactly, sir. Did you think you might browbeat me with impunity?"

"What feminine nonsense is this? Browbeat, indeed! I merely—"

"You merely attacked me the moment I walked into the room, quite ruining my good mood, I might add.

And though I perceive that being possessed of riches and good looks has quite spoiled you to the point where you believe you may ride roughshod over all you meet, allow me to inform you that—"

"Spoiled! Ride roughshod! My dear young woman, I am persuaded I have treated you with the utmost consideration. Consideration, I might add, that I had no call to bestow upon you. After all, this scheme was of your devising. It was you who came to me for help."

"Exactly," she said, "I came to you for help, not to be treated like the veriest widgeon who need not be consulted on matters that have every bearing upon her present and future life. Furthermore, I—"

She broke off abruptly. Her breathing was labored, causing her bosom to rise and fall as though she had been running, and while Nathan watched, she took several deep, steadying breaths, consciously bringing her emotions under control.

"Sir," she said at last, "I fear I have let my temper run away with me." Though her voice was much calmer, her bosom still rose and fell at an unnatural cadence.

"Well," he said, following her example in at least moderating his voice, "is that all the apology I am to receive?"

Her dark brown eyes lit with fire, but this time she kept a rein upon her tongue. After a moment of charged silence, she made him a polite curtsy, then said, "I bid you good evening, sir." With that, she turned and strode toward the door, her head held high and her back rigidly straight.

Nathan did not doubt for a minute her intention of leaving the room, nor her resolve not to return. He covered the room in half a dozen long strides, but her hand was already on the knob when he caught up with her. Stretching his arm past her shoulder, he pressed his palm solidly against the wood so that she was unable to open the door without a struggle.

Obviously perceiving the futility of such an act, she dropped her hand to her side. If he expected a show of humility, however, the continued rigidity of her back soon disabused him of that notion. Eugenia Bailey might be an impecunious schoolteacher, but she was far from humble. In fact, she was the most spirited woman Nathan had ever known—and the most stubborn. Of course, when he considered the matter, he *had* disappeared without offering her the least explanation, and though he was not in the habit of justifying his actions to anyone, perhaps there was a certain basis for her annoyance.

Not doubting for a moment that he could charm her into a return to her earlier happy disposition, he leaned his right shoulder against the door, effectively putting his face within inches of hers. After favoring her with a smile—the same smile countless women had referred to as "an unfair advantage"—he looked deeply into her eyes.

"So," he said, completely ignoring her remarks about his being spoiled and inconsiderate, "you think me a handsome fellow, do you?"

As he had expected, her cheeks grew quite pink. "Sir, I gave voice to much that would have been better left unsaid."

"Perhaps," he replied quietly, "but truth is often spoken in anger."

He could tell from the way she lowered her lashes that she was finding his closeness and this manner of conversing disturbing. Thinking to make her pay just a little more, he reached out and caught a curl that had come loose from her coiffure to lay against the side of her graceful neck. Like the curl, his knuckle brushed her smooth skin, and as he lifted the tress and slowly wound it around his finger, she made a soft, involuntary gasp.

"Is this the way you usually end arguments with females?" she asked, her voice a bit breathy.

"Truth to tell," he said, giving the curl a playful tug, "I have never argued with a female before. I never needed to."

At this, she lifted her gaze to his face. "A moment ago, when I let my tongue rule my head, did I happen to mention the word 'coxcomb'?"

It was as well for her that Nathan saw her lips twitch, otherwise he might have been obliged to turn the full force of his charm upon her, just to make her pay for that added piece of impertinence. "I said no more than the truth, madam, for I have never before argued with a female."

As he repeated the statement, it occurred to Nathan that a number of women in his keeping had given vent to their tempers. For the most part, however, he had merely ignored them or taken himself off; those women did not mean enough to him to put up with their tantrums. If this admission begged some sort of conclusion regarding Eugenia Bailey, Nathan chose to ignore it. Instead, he said, "Please, will you come back and allow me to pour you a glass of wine so that we may start this evening anew?"

When her eyes betrayed her, telling him that she wanted to do as he asked, he knew what was needed to convince her. Speaking softly, soothingly, he said, "You were correct in at least one thing."

"I was?" No more immune to his blandishments than any other woman, she added, "And what might that one thing be?"

"I should never have left you alone for . . . how many days, did you say?"

"Six," she replied, not resisting when he lifted her

hand and put it in the crook of his elbow, then escorted her back to the settee.

He is a total scoundrel, Eugenia told herself while she watched him pour her a glass of sherry. *A charming, devastatingly handsome scoundrel. And a woman with the least regard for her own well-being would not forget that fact!*

Armed with that warning, and resolved to heed it, she relaxed her guard enough so they were able to converse pleasantly for several minutes, until Riddle came to announce dinner. With the best will in the world, however, Eugenia could not still the flutter inside her midsection when Nathan took her hand once again to escort her to the dining room.

The meal was the most pleasant she had ever shared, and more than once Nathan made her laugh at some *on dit* concerning the visiting royals. "Her Imperial Highness, the Duchess of Oldenburg, is by far the most arrogant of our visitors," he said, "and she never lets anyone forget that she is sister to Tsar Alexander."

"And what of the Tsar?" Eugenia asked.

"I have met him only once, but on that occasion he was not a bit starched-up. Quite affable, in fact. He has become the center of a rather fanatical group of admirers, and each day crowds stand outside the Pulteney Hotel, hoping for a glimpse of him. I understand he often goes to the window to wave, whereupon the crowds cheer and call out his name."

Though Eugenia admitted that he sounded quite civil, she prayed she would not encounter him or his sister, the duchess, at the masked ball—not while she was dressed as a lightskirt! "Am I likely to meet any of the royals tomorrow night?"

"Who can say? With so many people invited, the visiting royals may feel the affair beneath their notice. I have it on good authority, however, that Prinny means to put in an appearance. His Royal Highness is quite jealous of the Tsar's popularity, and as a result, he is making every effort to endear himself to his subjects."

When Riddle chose that moment to set a cup and saucer and a small silver teapot next to Eugenia's plate, a special attention she had not requested, Nathan abandoned the subject of the ball. Instead, he asked the butler what he was doing.

"Begging your pardon, sir," Riddle replied, blandly turning the handle of the teapot so it was within her reach, "but Miss Eugenia enjoys a cup of tea with her sweet."

"Does she, now?"

Eugenia felt her face grow warm. She knew these little kindnesses were a result of the encounter with Fiona's "uncle," but she did not wish to speak of her part in that meeting for fear she might betray her knowledge of Nathan's heroic rescue of the child—a subject *he* might not wish to discuss.

After searching the butler's unrevealing face, then looking at Eugenia, who immediately busied herself with the pouring of the steaming, mahogany brew, Nathan asked no more questions. Instead, he told Riddle he would have his glass of port while the lady drank her tea.

"I shall be glad of the company," he said to her, "then afterward, perhaps we may adjourn to the drawing room for our lesson."

Unable to recall any mention earlier of another lesson, she looked at him, her eyebrows raised in question.

He smiled, apparently pleased to have caught her unawares. "If memory serves me, madam, you said you did not know how to waltz."

"Yes, I did, but—"

"Drink your tea," he said, interrupting before she could think of some excuse that would allow her to put off that particular lesson. Though it was not the instruction but the instructor she wished to avoid. For some reason, Nathan had decided to charm her, and since she was finding it disturbingly easy to allow herself to be charmed, she thought it best that she avoid the kind of close proximity required for the teaching of a dance.

While she drank the first cup of tea, and then the second, she racked her brain for a plausible excuse to retire to her bedchamber. Unfortunately, not even one idea presented itself, and before she knew it, Nathan was standing beside her chair, his hand held out to her.

"Come," he said, "let us waste no more time. Unless," he added softly, his gray eyes all but daring her to deny him, "you are afraid to be in a man's arms."

If an inability to draw breath into her lungs was anything to go by, she was most definitely afraid, yet the tumultuous beating of her heart would not let her give in to that fear.

"You are being absurd," she replied, just a bit too brightly. "I am not afraid."

The smile that teased his lips said he did not believe her. "Prove it," he said.

Feeling a kinship to a hapless rabbit outwitted by a very crafty fox, she placed her hand in Nathan's and let him lead her to the adjacent room.

"I should like to know," he said, once she had disposed herself upon the settee, "how you managed to turn Riddle up sweet in the few days since I saw you last."

Still not wanting to discuss that encounter, she shrugged her shoulders, as if she had not the least idea, and when he gave her a look that said he was not deceived, she changed the subject by inquiring of him how they were to waltz without music.

"Nothing easier," he replied, taking her hand and bringing her to her feet. "Compared to the country dances, the figures of the waltz are quite simple, little more than step-step-close, step-step-close, but the pattern is best learned without the lure of the music."

"Lure? A strange choice of word, sir."

"Tell me that, madam, after you have mastered the basics and been pulled inextricably into the three-four time. I promise you, the experience is compelling."

Not more than ten minutes later, Eugenia would have argued that "compelling" was too tame a word. If asked to describe the experience of waltzing with Nathan Seymour, she would have called it nothing less than exhilarating.

The basic box step was easily mastered, requiring no more than one or two false starts. It was the feel of Nathan's arm around her waist that left Eugenia all but speechless and brought that flutter back to her midsection. Then he began to hum a waltz tune, sweeping her into an ever-widening circle while matching their steps to the dum-da-da, dum-da-da of his tune, and she understood what me meant about being pulled into the music.

No wonder this dance was so controversial!

It was titillating enough that a man and a woman remained with one partner the entire time, facing one another with scarce ten inches of space between their bodies. But those things were not the real threat to morality. The true danger lay in the rhythm. It pulled a person into its pulsating beat. There was something intoxicating about moving in perfect step with one's partner—dipping and swaying to the music—and something decidedly primal about having to follow a gentleman's lead, aware of his strength, obliged to match one's own sense of rhythm to his until you felt the two of you were in perfect harmony.

This primal sensation was compounded if the gentleman was a scoundrel who gazed into a lady's eyes, all the while twirling her faster and faster until she was obliged to endure his holding her ever closer to keep her from spinning into oblivion. Almost dizzy with the whirling and Nathan's humming and the feel of his strong arm keeping her from harm, she did not protest when he drew her even closer and lifted her feet right off the ground.

It was no more than self-preservation when she slipped her left arm up around his broad shoulders and held tightly to him. Similarly, it was eminently reasonable, when he finally ended the song and the dance, that she continued to hold on to him, lest she fall.

While they stood thus, Eugenia heard the sound of her labored breathing, but whether that difficulty resulted from the unaccustomed exercise of the dance or the fact that her breasts were pressed against Nathan's rock-hard chest, she could not say. All she knew for certain was that she was but a hairbreadth from putting her other arm around his shoulders and leaning even closer to him.

He seemed to read her thoughts, for he drew her that final bit closer. After gazing into her eyes, silently asking a question whose answer she must have given, he slowly dipped his head toward hers. Of their own volition, her eyelids closed, and Eugenia waited for the touch of Nathan's lips upon hers, every inch of her skin tingling with awareness as she felt the warmth of him coming ever nearer.

His mouth was poised to claim hers when the knocker sounded on the entrance door, startling Eugenia into opening her eyes. The harsh echo of the heavy brass being pounded repeatedly against the knocker plate seemed to rouse her from what was surely bewitchment, and she pushed against Nathan's chest, moving, albeit reluctantly, out of his arms.

"Damnation!" Nathan muttered. "Whoever that is, he will not live to see another day."

Suddenly burning with embarrassment, Eugenia hurried to the other side of the room. "Nathan, I—"

"Nate, old boy," Mr. Martin Winfield called from the vestibule, "you in there?"

Not bothering to knock, the gentleman opened the door and entered the drawing room, excitement lending high color to his ever-affable face. "I have had the most amazing evening at the whist table, Nate. You will not credit it, not with my usual poor luck at cards, but I won a pony off Fothagill and a stack of yellow boys from George and Harold. Knew you would be happy for me, so I decided to come around and fetch you before I went to White's. Thought you might like to see me in action before my luck runs out."

"It just did," Nathan said, his tone noticeably vexed.

Oblivious to both the tone and the comment, the smiling gentleman came forward and took Eugenia's hand, lifting it to his lips with a practiced air. "Good evening, Miss Eugenia. You will have no objection, I am sure, if I take Nathan off with me."

"No, no," she said somewhat unevenly. "No objections at all. As it happens, I was just taking my leave. It has been a long and rather eventful day, and I find I am grown tired."

Having said this, she turned to Nathan, keeping her eyes downcast, and curtsied. "Good night, sir. Thank you for the lesson."

When Nathan said nothing, she offered her hand once again to Mr. Winfield, who kissed it, then escorted her to the door. "Sweet repose," he said, but before she could reply he had turned back to Nathan. "Nate, I wish you could have seen the look on Fothagill's face when he knew I had bested him. It was enough to—" The door closed and Eugenia heard no more.

To her regret, Riddle had remained in the vestibule, and at sight of her he hurried to the cherry console table to light one of the tapers. "Here you are, Miss Eugenia," he said, handing over the bed candle. "May I wish you pleasant dreams?"

The butler's good wishes came too late, for Eugenia had just been wakened from her dream. She thanked him, however, and took the candle, marveling that her hand did not tremble, revealing her inner turmoil. She did not linger on the stairs, but climbed them with all haste. Only when she was in her bedchamber, the door closed behind her, did she let herself think of the kiss that had almost happened, the kiss Martin Winfield had interrupted.

She had wanted Nathan to kiss her—wanted it with all her heart—but now that she was away from him, away from the mesmerizing effect of the waltz and the feel of his muscular arms circling her waist, she was relieved the kiss had not happened. Nathan Seymour was a man whose conquests were legion, and chances were good that he could not even remember all the women he had kissed. In all likelihood, one more might have been equally forgettable.

It was a lowering thought. Lowering, but nonetheless true. And what if Nathan *had* kissed her, and afterward she had made a fool of herself, giving the act more importance than it deserved? How would she have faced him the next day?

Telling herself she had been spared a very embarrassing situation, Eugenia began to disrobe. Unmindful of the cruel treatment to her scalp, she yanked the combs from her hair, tossing the combs and her clothing on the floor in a manner that was totally out of character with her usual neatness. Soon her knees began to shake, and, afraid they might buckle beneath her, she threw herself upon the bed, her face buried in the pillow.

If a sob caught in her throat, then escaped her lips as she recalled the sensation of being pressed against Nathan's chest, it was no wonder. After acknowledging that a kiss between them might have meant nothing to him, she was obliged to admit that it would have meant the world to her.

Chapter Eight

Most of the next day was spent preparing for the long-awaited masked ball, and Eugenia did not see Nathan until that evening when she descended the stairs, dressed and ready to step into the carriage. Not that she had wanted to see him. Still uncertain about her own feelings, she feared she might see in him a look of relief that he had escaped a possibly embarrassing entanglement with a spinster schoolteacher.

Not wanting to put her luck to the test, she had remained in her room.

About midafternoon a self-important little man known as Monsieur Jacques arrived to arrange Eugenia's hair. After washing and drying the long, thick strands, then treating them with a glycerine that brought out the red highlights in her brown tresses, the Frenchman arranged the whole atop her head, with a waterfall effect of ringlets brushing the nape of her neck.

Eugenia cared little for the elegant coiffure, and later she dressed without the least appreciation for the expensive emerald green satin of the ball gown. The material was exquisite, and when she moved, it swished like a spring wind rustling through the trees; however, Eugenia scarcely noticed. She was becoming heartily sick of the blatant exposure of her bosom and the lack of subtlety in the design of the borrowed gowns.

After applying lip rouge and another of the heart-shaped patches, she bid the chambermaid thread the ribbons of the satin half mask through Monsieur Jacques's elaborately arranged handiwork. "Knot the ties," she said, adjusting the swansdown-trimmed disguise more comfortably over her eyes, "for I shall not remove the mask until I return to the town house."

Allowing the maid to place the matching green domino upon her shoulders, Eugenia fastened the intricately corded gold frogs to secure the long, flowing cape. With nothing more to detain her, she bid the servant not wait up for her, then quit the room. The rustling of her finery accompanied each step, and when she descended the stairs to join Nathan, who waited in the vestibule, his muscular physique handsomely encased in beautifully cut evening clothes of unrelieved black, the unmistakable whisper of satin caused her escort to turn and regard her progress toward him.

He met her at the bottom step, and though his eyes told her he liked what he saw, he offered her no compliments—a fact for which Eugenia was most grateful. Instead, he merely took her hand and led her to the cherry console upon which lay a black leather jeweler's box. "I should have sent these up," he said, opening the box to reveal a gold filigree necklace from which hung a diamond pendant—a handsome stone that reflected the candles in the chandelier, and sparkled with blue, green, and yellow fire. Also reposing in the velvet-lined bed of the box were matching teardrop earrings and a slender filigree bracelet.

Harlots' wages, Eugenia thought.

"You will need to remove your domino to don the necklace," Nathan said.

Wishing she need not do so, but understanding that the jewelry was nothing more than the trappings of the role she played, she released the braided frogs and allowed the butler to take the long cape. Without a word, Nathan placed the necklace around Eugenia's throat. It felt heavy and cold to her skin, as did the bracelet.

Ignoring the looking glass that hung above the console table, she fitted the posts of the earrings into her lobes then allowed the butler to return the domino to her shoulders. "I am ready," she said, refastening the frogs.

Nathan had watched her don the bracelet and earrings, and though she refrained from comment of any kind, he knew she was not pleased with the jewelry. This was certainly a first! Until tonight, he had never bestowed even the most insignificant trinket upon a female without her rushing to see her reflection in a looking glass. As well, those other women's appreciation for such gifts had always been effusive and ultimately expressed more fully in milady's bedchamber.

Not that he had expected that ultimate show of appreciation from Eugenia. He had, however, envisioned some slight indication of her pleasure in the gift. After all, it was not as though she had a box filled with such baubles. Obviously she would have preferred not to open the box before the servants—she was quite proud—but he had already acknowledged his carelessness in not sending them up to her earlier. What more did she want? Did she have to act, for all the world, as though she were embarrassed?

Deciding that he had done nothing for which he needed to apologize, Nathan followed Eugenia outside and helped her into the landau, and within moments they were on their way to Burlington House, the site of the ball. If they traveled the distance in total silence, that was her choice.

Under normal circumstances, the drive from Grosvenor Square to Bond Street, then south to Burlington House required but a matter of minutes, but on that particular night, it appeared that every carriage in London was on the road. The resulting traffic moved at a snail's crawl, and it was a full hour before they reached their destination and another ten minutes before the coachman pulled up to the front entrance of the magnificent Palladian-style house.

The walk was roped off on either side of the entrance, and beadles and guards hired especially for the occasion patrolled the streets that bordered Burlington House, their purpose to keep the crowds of gawkers from pushing too close to the invited guests. As well, Bow Street runners milled about, their job to watch for those daring souls who might break free of the throngs and attempt to snatch jewelry from the ladies attending the ball.

"Oh, my," Eugenia said, finally breaking the silence that had prevailed since they entered the carriage. "I had not thought the place would be so big."

"I had not thought there would be so many people," Nathan replied, stepping down to the pavement, then turning to offer her his hand. He looked at the unbroken line of carriages coming south on Bond Street and the line that clogged Piccadilly from both the east and the west. "Two thousand were invited. From the looks of it, however, I should think there are twice that many either already inside or trying to make their way here."

After donning a black silk mask, he gave Eugenia his arm and led her up the broad stairs and into the large, brightly lit vestibule, where he showed his invitation to the majordomo. Hundreds of candles shone from the massive crystal chandelier above their heads, and double that number burned in the many sconces placed all along the walls. The fragrance of melting wax blended with the perfumes of the throng of people already inside the house, and the combination of sweet and spicy aromas filled the air.

Pausing only long enough to give her domino into the hands of a waiting footman, Nathan and Eugenia made their way up the central grand staircase, joining guests dressed in costumes and finery of every color. One of them, a gentleman with a club foot, was dressed as a rather sinister-looking monk, and if Eugenia had not heard a young lady nearby whisper to her escort that it was Lord Byron, she might have been frightened.

The celebrated poet was not the only guest with a flair for the dramatic. Farther up the stairs was a lady whose Medusa wig, at first glance, looked enough like real snakes to send a shiver down Eugenia's back. At least, she *thought* the person was a lady. If revealing clothes and painted faces were anything to judge by, Eugenia was not the only female there whose virtue might be in question, and many a lady and gentleman nodded at Nathan, who had discarded his mask, then turned away when their glances fell upon his companion.

For his part, Nathan merely returned their nods, placing his hand over Eugenia's where it rested on his arm. "Remember your purpose in attending this affair," he said, "and keep your head up high."

"Yes," she replied, complying with his suggestion, yet grateful for his strong arm and his emotional support, "I will remember."

Once they had greeted the Earl of Burlington and his hostess, plus those members of White's who constituted the welcoming committee, they separated from the masses who continued toward the public rooms where refreshments and champagne were to be found. Seeking someplace less packed with humanity, Nathan and Eugenia strolled to the exhibition galleries to view the earl's extensive art collection.

The works of Reynolds, Gainsborough, and Turner abounded, as well as those by Vandyke and Reubens. Paintings by the old masters hung beside those of the new masters, and Eugenia stood for some time before a portrait of Henry VIII, by Holbein. Later, she appeared quite enthralled by a Rembrandt oil on canvas known as *Man with a Magnifying Glass*.

With a sigh of pure enjoyment, she said, "If Rembrandt had given us nothing more, that painting alone was deed enough to leave the world a better place for his having lived upon it."

Recalling their conversation about what Eugenia's mother had taught her, Nathan said, "Ah, yes, number four, I believe, among the 'essential lessons.'"

As more people entered the gallery, rendering the space uncomfortably crowded, he cupped her elbow and led her down the stairs to the ballroom, where the musicians had struck up the opening quadrille. "And what of you?" he asked. "What deed will you perform, do you think?"

"Who can say? I do not think most of us can plan our deed, not unless we are dedicated to some cause or other. I think the deed is often an accident. Something happens suddenly, and a person lives up to the demands of the moment or he does not. As was the case with you."

Nathan was taken aback. "Me? I assure you, I have done nothing noteworthy.

"But you have," she said, an almost shy quality to her voice. "You saved Fiona."

"No, no. I merely caught a child who was on the brink of falling from a second-story window. Anyone would have done the same."

"But anyone did not. Furthermore," she added, "you helped that child escape. Then you involved yourself in her well-being by giving her employment and making certain she was safe and well fed."

"But that was nothing, I assure you."

She shook her head. "It may have been nothing to you, but it was life itself for Fiona. I . . . I think you were very heroic, and I am pleased to have known you."

Nathan could not believe the dichotomous feelings of

pleasure and embarrassment he felt at her words. On the one hand, he was pleased she no longer thought him a complete scoundrel, but on the other hand, he had done nothing heroic where the little maid was concerned. If the truth be known, he was in his cups the night he spied her climbing out that window, and only after he had caught her did he realize she was escaping from one of those most despicable of places, a brothel where children were forced into prostitution.

If anyone was brave, it was Fiona for attempting the escape, and Eugenia for protecting the little girl from that lout who entered the town house and threatened her with a knife. When Nathan had heard of the incident only this morning, he had been appalled. Still filled with rage at the very thought of what might have happened, he felt his hands ball into fists, and he longed to confront that fellow, Weems, so he might rearrange his face.

Nathan said none of this, however, for they had reached the two-story marble columns that guarded the entrance to the flower-bedecked ballroom, and immediately the moment was missed. Martin Winfield appeared to have been waiting for them, and he waved them over to where he stood near an ivy-festooned wall sconce.

"Nate," he greeted with his usual affability, "good to see you, old boy."

He bowed over Eugenia's hand. "As for you, ma'am, I have been waiting this age to claim you for the first dance. I hope you have not forgotten you promised it to me."

"I have not forgotten, sir. But I believe ours was to be the first *waltz*, was it not?"

"In which case," said a masked gentleman dressed from head to toe in gold, from his gold mask and coat down to his satin knee britches and his gold-painted evening slippers, "I claim the honor of joining in the quadrille with the lady who is *not* named Rose." He bowed before Eugenia: "Alvin Comstock, at your service, ma'am. We met in the park the other day."

"I remember you, sir," Eugenia said, holding up her finger, "even without the aid of a string."

The gentleman laughed aloud. "Jolly good of you, ma'am." Apparently taking this reference to their earlier conversation as proof of his acceptability as a partner, he placed Eugenia's hand upon his arm. As he led her onto the dance floor, she heard Nathan ask Winny the significance of Comstock's costume.

"Thinks he is King Midas," Winny replied. "Told him it was *other* items Midas turned to gold, but you know Comstock always was a slowtop."

Thankfully, the gentleman in gold seemed not to hear Winny's remark, and whatever Nathan's reply, it was lost in the noise of the room. Meanwhile, Eugenia and her partner joined a group in need of another pair, and if her arrival was greeted rather frostily by the lady to her right, she tried to disregard the reaction. Within moments, all else was forgotten as she became caught up in the figures of the quadrille.

She danced the next two sets with costumed gentlemen whose identities remained a mystery, and, as the evening wore on, she wondered why Nathan did not ask to partner her. Though she caught glimpses of him in conversation with a breathtaking young beauty in silver-spangled white gauze, and later with a rather animated dark-haired damsel in celestial blue silk, he did not dance with either lady. It was as though he had dedicated himself to leaning nonchalantly against the wall so he might observe her.

The nonchalance was deceptive; beneath it was a subtle wariness that surfaced when Eugenia was returned to his side only to be approached within the instant by a tall, slender man with dark, wavy hair. The man's still-handsome face was only partially concealed by the black leather mask that was his only concession to the theme of the evening, but Eugenia would have known who he was had his visage been completely covered. Nothing could disguise those coal black eyes—eyes that stared overlong at her décolletage, making her yearn to give him the snub he deserved and turn her back to him.

She did not turn, however. Instead, she called upon the lesson that had served her before and gave him the briefest of smiles before lowering her lashes.

"The little bookworm," the man said, bowing over her hand. "Well met, ma'am. May I say you look magnificent this evening?"

"Durham," Nathan said before Eugenia could respond to the fulsome compliment.

"Seymour," his lordship replied, returning Nathan's cool greeting. "Dare I request the honor of a dance with your beautiful protégée?"

Nathan raised a questioning eyebrow. "*Dare?* A strange choice of word, my lord."

"Not at all, sir. I should not wish to find myself called out for, shall we say, poaching on private preserves."

Though Eugenia cringed at Lord Durham's remark, which made her sound less like a human and more like a specie of animal life owned by Nathan Seymour, she was far more concerned by the looks that passed between the two men. There was an undercurrent of animosity she had not expected, and if intensity was anything to judge by, the enmity was of long duration.

Thinking it wise to separate them before they drew the attention of those guests standing nearby, she touched Lord Durham's arm, placing her fingers lightly upon his sleeve. "If we do not join the lines now, my lord, the places will all be filled."

Almost reluctantly, he returned his attention to Eugenia. "Ah, yes, lovely lady."

Without another word, he caught her hand and put it in

the crook of his arm; then, with a studied carelessness, he nodded in Nathan's direction, and led Eugenia toward the crowd of dancers.

Though she wondered what could have caused the obvious abhorrence felt by both Nathan and Lord Durham, she reminded herself it was none of her concern. Her concern was reclaiming her cousin Thad's ten thousand pounds, and to do that it was imperative she charm Lord Durham sufficiently to convince him to play cards with her. With her goal foremost in her mind, she decided to abandon the role of coy young miss. Cedric Durham was no fool, and surely such a man would find too much coyness a bore. "Is your feud with Nathan Seymour of long duration, my lord?"

Somewhat taken aback by the question, he stared at her, almost as if attempting to see beneath the swansdown mask. "So," he drawled, "the little bookworm is curious about more than literature. Do you think that altogether wise? Did you never hear what curiosity did for the cat?"

She smiled, as though his question were no more than amusing repartee. "And did you never hear of mixed metaphors, my lord? You cannot have it both ways. I am either a bookworm, or I am a cat. I fear you must choose one or the other."

He leaned very close, whispering in her ear. "And if I choose neither? What if there is something else I should wish to call you?"

Eugenia wanted nothing so much as to wipe her gloved hand across her ear to remove the feel of his hot breath upon her skin, but she resisted the temptation. Instead, she touched the diamond pendant that rested inside the hollow of her throat. "You may call me whatever you wish, my lord, but I shall hope it is something a bit more flattering than a paste-eating larva. Perhaps a butterfly or a bird. I should like to be a bird, for they make such beautiful music."

They had found a place at the end of the line and waited only for the orchestra to commence playing. "And do you make beautiful music?" he asked. "In which case, I might call you my nightingale."

"Alas," she said, emphasizing her words with a dramatic sigh, "I am not at all musical. My ability at the pianoforte is mediocre at best, and not even the least discerning listener could find pleasure in my singing."

He spoke close to her ear again, his voice low, insinuating. "If what you say is true, one must suppose that you can boast other, more interesting, talents."

Choosing to misunderstand him, she said, "I never boast, my lord, but I flatter myself that I am not totally without redeeming qualities."

Lord Durham slipped his forefinger beneath the diamond pendant, forcing Eugenia to grit her teeth when his fingertips came into contact with her skin. "If this little bauble is any indication," he said, admiring the reflection of the candlelight in the gem, "you must, indeed, possess redeeming qualities. Unless I am mistaken, I saw this very necklace not three days ago at Rundall and Bridges, where, if one is interested in such information, I was told it could be had for a mere thousand pounds."

A thousand pounds! Eugenia was human enough to find that *very* interesting. As an instructress who earned thirty pounds per annum, she vowed to be less hasty in the future about ridiculing harlots' wages.

Thankfully, the orchestra struck up the chords for the Lancers, and Durham had, perforce, to take his place, making any but the briefest of comments impossible. Once, when they joined hands for several seconds, Durham asked her about those *other* talents. "If, as you say, you are not musical, then, pray, in what manner do you occupy your time?"

Her reply was postponed until they came together again, but the delay gave her time to consider her answer.

This was the moment she had been waiting for, and when they joined hands again, she smiled up at him, hoping to convince him that she had nothing more consequential in mind than social chit-chat. "In answer to your question, my lord, I have many interests. I paint and, as you know, I enjoy reading. Oh, and I am excessively fond of playing cards."

"Cards, you say?"

She nodded. "There are those who say I play rather well."

"Do they now?" he said, his bland tone implying nothing more than polite interest.

With that, Eugenia was forced to be content, for they were separated once again. When the final strains of the music had sounded, Durham reclaimed her, placed her hand upon his arm, and led her from the dance floor. If he had found her disclosure regarding her fondness for cards of interest, he kept the fact to himself. Instead, he said, "Tell me, my mysterious one, if I were to send you a nosegay to thank you for this dance, to whom should I direct it?"

Still hoping to keep her identity a secret, she laughed lightly in what she hoped was a coquettish manner. "A nosegay? How thoughtful of you, my lord. As it happens, I am excessively fond of flowers."

"Your name?" he prompted.

"Oh," she replied, "why do you not pen the card, 'To a butterfly,' for did we not decide that was a more fitting appellation than nightingale?"

"So," he said, "you persist in keeping your identity a secret. Very well, *Papillion*. But is your residence to remain a mystery as well? May I not know your direction?"

Even in the presence of such a scoundrel as this, the answer to that last question brought the heat to Eugenia's face.

As if sensing her hesitancy, he said, "Am I not to be allowed to pay you a visit?"

"For the time being, my lord, I think visits might be a bit awkward."

"And why is that? Has Seymour got you on such a short leash you may not entertain whom you please in your own drawing room?"

"I . . . I have no drawing room at present, for I am staying at Nathan's town house in Grosvenor Square."

"Ecod! Never tell me Seymour has set you up in his home!"

She had his interest now. Unfortunately, she realized too late that she had revealed something she would have done better to keep to herself. "I am there only for the moment," she said. "In a fortnight, I shall be resettling in an establishment more suited to my lifestyle." She failed to inform him that the establishment was the Misses Becknell's Academy for Young Females, but even if she had done so, she doubted he would have heard her. He seemed to be lost in his own thoughts.

A smile that had nothing to do with mirth pulled at his lips, revealing small, slightly pointed teeth. "Seymour has brass, I will give him that, to keep his fancy piece in Grosvenor Square. 'Twould be interesting to discover if the more high-minded of the neighborhood share my view upon the subject. Very interesting, indeed."

Before Eugenia could think of anything to rectify the mistake she had made, Durham returned her to Nathan's side, bowed over her hand, and disappeared into the crowd.

Within minutes of her return, Nathan suggested they leave the ball. Since Eugenia had accomplished that for which she came—to further her acquaintance with Lord Durham—she was more than willing to leave. She said nothing of her conversation with his lordship until she and Nathan were in the landau once again, inching their way past the seemingly unending stream of carriages still attempting to deliver their passengers to the ball.

It had needed half an hour for the coachman to make his way around to the courtyard at the rear of Burlington House, where departing guests were met, and in that time, Nathan had asked no questions about her dance with Durham, and Eugenia had offered no comments. To her relief, the carriage was announced before Nathan had finished calling her attention to those architectural features that distinguished the rear of Lord Burlington's impressive mansion.

"Well," he said some twenty minutes later when they had at last turned onto Upper Grosvenor Street, "do you mean to keep me wondering forever what transpired between you and Durham?"

"I told him I did not play the pianoforte," she said.

"And?"

"I told him I played cards instead. And before you berate me, allow me to inform you that I introduced the topic with the utmost subtlety."

Dismissing her show of defensiveness, Nathan asked, "What was Durham's response to this disclosure?"

"Who can say with such a man? His reaction was much the same as if I had just told him I preferred lemon in my tea."

"He was not interested?"

"Not in that," she replied, and though she tried to keep her tone even, something in her voice betrayed her.

"If not in that," Nathan asked far too quietly, "in what *was* he interested?"

Eugenia cleared her throat. "Lord Durham seemed rather intrigued by the information that I am a guest at Grosvenor Square."

"You told him you were staying at my house!"

She nodded. "I am sorry, Nathan, but I find I am not as good at dissembling as I had thought. I was busy trying to avoid telling him my name, and as a result, when he asked my direction, I could think of nothing but the truth."

"Drat the fellow! I should have known he would try to discover where you lived. Any woman under my protection becomes an object of pursuit for Durham."

Choosing not to take exception to being lumped with his lights of love, she said, "Have I put you in an awkward position?"

"Me? Not at all. I care little if my neighbors turn up their noses. You, however, might find it unpleasant should a committee of incensed busybodies begin beating upon the door and demanding to know why I had a female in my house."

At the thought, Eugenia experienced a feeling of uneasiness in the pit of her stomach. "Might that happen?"

"I hope not, but Durham will make mischief for me if he can, and he will care little who else is made uncomfortable."

Eugenia said nothing, but merely listened to the metallic ring of the horses' shoes as they struck the cobblestone street, wondering all the while how she had concocted the hare-brained notion of charming Lord Durham into playing cards with her. Such arrogance, to think she could best that particular scoundrel. When it came to duplicity, she was an amateur and his lordship was a seasoned professional.

"Perhaps," Nathan said, interrupting her fruitless repining, "it is possible to cheat Durham of his petty victory. Of course, if we are to do so, it behooves us to quit the town house before first light. Can you be ready to leave with only a few hours' notice?"

"Of course. I can be packed and ready to return to the school within the hour."

"The school? Whatever for? You will go with me to

Hertfordshire, of course. I thought we had settled all that the evening Winny dined with us."

"We did not. As usual, you issued a decree and expected it to be obeyed. I chose to disregard it. I still choose to do so."

"You would return to the Misses Buckram merely because of my decree, as you call it? If you were so miffed, why did you not simply ring a peal over me? You have certainly done it before."

"Becknell," she corrected. "And I have never rung a peal over you." Though she knew the statement to be untrue, she persevered. "As a guest in your home, I would never act in such an unladylike manner."

"Remind me," he said, his tone spuriously bland, "to return to that particular whisker at some later date. For now, allow me to extend an invitation to you in the most civil manner possible. Madam, will you accompany me to my home in Hertfordshire?"

She shook her head. "I cannot—not without a chaperone. You must see that."

"I see nothing of the sort. We have no chaperone here, and such attention to the proprieties at this late date smells strongly of missishness."

"It is not missishness. Furthermore, the circumstances are not at all the same."

"What is so different about your accompanying me to the country?"

"Here," she said, "we are shielded somewhat by the anonymity that prevails in a populous city. Or we were before this evening. In the country, where people are few and where Mr. Nathan Seymour is recognized as a principal figure in the neighborhood, the situation would be quite different. Should you bring an unchaperoned lady to your estate, the entire population would be scandalized, and rightly so. Besides . . ."

"Besides?"

She could not stop the sigh that escaped her. "I find I am heartily sick of playing the part of your mistress. I wish to be me—in my own clothes and with my own—"

"Then do not come as my mistress," he said, his voice clipped, as though he wished to put an end to the discussion. "Come as anything you like."

He sat rigidly against the squabs of the coach, his face turned to the window, his attention focused on something unseen, something beyond the darkness of the night. He said nothing more until the horses came to a stop before the town house. As Eugenia gathered her things in preparation to alight, he leaned forward and caught her hand. "Forgive me," he said, his voice surprisingly quiet.

The closeness of the carriage, plus his softly spoken apology and the warmth of his strong hand holding hers, caused a feeling of such intimacy between them that Eugenia had difficulty catching her breath.

"Come to Hertfordshire with me," he said, the words little more than a whisper. "I should like to show you my home."

"But, I—"

"Please," he said. "Wear whatever makes you comfortable, but come with me . . . as my friend."

Chapter Nine

Come as my friend. Eugenia had been unable to ignore the softly spoken request. If the truth be told, she had not wanted to ignore it.

She had been at the Misses Becknell's Academy for seven years, and in that time, she had sorely missed the peace and quiet of the country, not to mention the relative freedom of being where one's every move was not observed and judged. Restricted by the circumspect behavior required of an instructress, and by the somewhat narrow code of conduct embraced by her elderly employers, Eugenia longed to be free to take solitary walks without anyone questioning her whereabouts or the length of time she meant to be away.

The thought of such freedom was too enticing to resist, and Eugenia agreed to go to Swanleigh Hall. She pushed to the back of her mind the breathlessness she felt at that moment, with Nathan's hand holding hers and his whispered plea all but filling the intimate darkness of the coach. Not for an instant did she admit to herself that she wanted very much to accompany him to his home—wanted to be in his company—wanted to be his friend.

The next day the two friends climbed aboard the carriage while the sun was still little more than a promise, and only a few pink streaks lightened the still gray sky. By the time the day was an established fact, the crowded streets of London had given way to the peace of the country roads. The trip to St. Albans required little more than three hours, and the remaining six miles to Stanton-on-Lee needed less than half an hour. Traveling as they were in a well-sprung coach, the miles seemed to fly by, and Eugenia was almost sorry to see the experience end.

She thought Hertfordshire a beautiful county, with its leafy lanes and neat, prosperous village greens, and to add to the interest, every now and then an unexpected stone column or a stretch of ancient wall appeared, reminding Eugenia that Roman cities once covered the countryside. As they traveled, they passed small herds of deer, their graceful heads raised in sudden alarm at the passing carriage. They also saw several stretches of old coppiced woodlands, where hornbeam, oak, and birch trees strove to replenish themselves by sending their shoots skyward. And everywhere farms and grazing sheep abounded.

"It is lovely country," she said.

"Yes," Nathan agreed. "I miss it when I am gone for too long a time."

If Eugenia thought this a strange comment, she kept her opinion to herself. After all, where was it written that a man reputed to be a scoundrel could not love his home—or despise another scoundrel?

For almost the entire time since their early morning departure from London, Eugenia had wanted to ask Nathan about the animosity that existed between him and Lord Durham. She had thought of little else during the few hours she had lain upon her bed the night before, yet she knew if Cedric Durham had not wanted to tell her about the feud, Nathan would probably be equally reticent.

Still, she felt she had a right to know, for whatever existed between the two men might have an effect upon her ability to get Durham to play cards with her. With that justification in mind, she determined to discover the source of their animosity. As the coach passed through the pretty village of Stanton-on-Lee, with its charming timber-framed shops and its mud-and-timber cottages, most dating from the Tudor period, Eugenia gave her surroundings only a cursory look. Instead, she broached the subject of the feud.

"Is Lord Durham's home nearby," she asked, "or did you meet him elsewhere?"

"I met him at Eton," Nathan replied, his tone not inviting further questions.

Eugenia did not allow herself to be dissuaded. "He is older than you, I believe."

Nathan sighed. Then, as if giving in to the inevitable, he said, "Durham was two forms ahead of me."

"Did you dislike him immediately, or—"

"For a new boy, the older boys fall into two categories: those one admires and those one dislikes."

"And Durham fell into the latter category?"

"Decidedly."

Eugenia watched Nathan's eyes; they appeared gray and cold as a winter's day, and it was obvious that his thoughts were back at Eton.

"I do not know the traditions prevailing in a female academy," he said, "but for a boy, his first year at school can be a miserable experience."

"For a girl at school," Eugenia said, "there is bad food, lumpy beds, and cold classrooms, but the thing that provokes the most tears is homesickness. Sometimes, if a girl complains enough in her letters, her parents will come take her home."

"Lucky girls," Nathan said. "Such complaints do not succeed with a lad."

Perceiving a bitterness in his voice, she said, "Why is that?"

"Because a lad's parents expect the food to be bad and the rooms to be cold; furthermore, they expect the teachers to dispense swift and unswerving punishment. If one fails to conjugate one's Latin verbs, the reward is a firm swat or two with the instructor's cane."

Eugenia was incredulous. "A caning for nothing more than an error in declining a verb? Surely there must be some less severe form of punishment, one more suited to the offense?"

He shook his head. "Actually, those things the boy finds most detestable about the place are the very reasons he was sent to school. The parents—in most instances that means the fathers—want the lad to learn sportsmanship and fair play. They want him to learn to obey orders before he is allowed to give them, and they expect him to learn to persevere under unpleasant conditions. For those lessons, they depend upon the instructors in the classrooms, and outside the classrooms they depend upon the fag system."

His eyebrows lifted in question. "Do you understand about fags?"

"I have heard the word, but I am not certain what it means."

"Each new boy is assigned to an older boy and becomes known as his fag. In theory, the older boy takes the younger under his wing and teaches him the rules of the school. In actuality, the fag often becomes a sort of dogsbody, a drudge who must obey the older boy's orders. In some instances, this involves nothing more than fetching a forgotten schoolbook or carrying messages back and forth between friends. If the service is not performed correctly or in a timely manner, the fag is assigned some chore, such as polishing the older boy's shoes or emptying his slops."

He paused for a moment. "There are those who should never have power over others. It corrupts them. Such was the case with Cedric Durham. Durham treated his fag, a youngster with the unfortunate name of Partridge, worse than a serf. The lad was small for his age, with overlarge ears and a lock of hair that often stood on end, refusing to be subdued, and Durham delighted in ridiculing him before his peers, referring to him as Partridge Feathers."

Nathan's lips formed a thin, almost angry line. "Not content with humiliating the boy, Durham became physically abusive. When a job was not done to his specifications, he knocked the boy down, often kicking him or hitting him with his fists."

Eugenia gasped. "How monstrous of Durham, and how wretched for the poor little boy. Did no one inform the headmaster of this abuse?"

Nathan gave her a look that said hers was an idiotic question. "One does not tell. It simply is not done."

"What lunacy! If no one tells, how can a wrong be righted?"

"An interesting question," he said. "I should like to hear you pose it to the bagwig, though I already know his answer."

"Which would be?"

"He would puff up, insulted by the question, and reply, 'Tradition, madam. I will thank you not to trifle with tradition.'"

Eugenia made a sound of disgust. "We once had a tradition of drawing and quartering condemned felons and hanging their severed bodies from the four corners of London Bridge. Thankfully, someone trifled with that tradition!"

Having given vent to her anger, she returned to the subject at hand. "What became of the poor little boy? Did no one come to his aid?"

"Winny did. Or as much as was within the power of a youngster who was no bigger than the lad in question. He and Partridge were in the same form."

"Good for Mr. Winfield. He was very brave to champion his classmate. Whom did he tell?"

"He told me," Nathan replied. His voice was strangely emotionless, almost as if the telling of the story was dredging up memories he normally kept under strict control. "One day Winny came to me, asking if I could do something to stop the abuse."

"Was Winny your fag?"

Nathan seemed almost not to hear her. "What? Oh, yes, of course he was. That is how we met."

"But you and Winny are such close friends now. Obviously you did not find it necessary to punch or kick him."

"Oh, Lord, no! I am no bully. I was, however, tall for my age, and quite good at sports; and not a little pugnacious. No one ever bothered me, not even when I was a fag myself."

Looking at the tall, muscular man before her, Eugenia could well imagine that even as a boy Nathan Seymour possessed those qualities that inspired respect in other boys. "Did you stop Durham from abusing the poor Partridge boy?"

For a minute she thought he meant not to reply, then with a sigh he said, "I told Winny I would have a talk with Durham, make him see the error of his ways. I knew a bully like Durham would not listen to reason, but I was not afraid to fight him. Only . . ."

He stared at his hands, which were balled into fists. "Only I had a cricket match that Saturday afternoon, the last match of the season, and I knew if I should injure my hands, I would not be able to play. For that reason, I told Winny I would take care of the matter after the match."

From the dullness of his voice, Eugenia could tell Nathan was reliving the incident, and that for some reason he felt guilty about the outcome. "What happened?" she asked, keeping her own voice quiet. "Did you speak to Durham after the match?"

"No. By then it was too late. That Friday evening, after a particularly cruel jest played on him by Durham, young

Partridge tore his bedsheet into strips, plaited the strips together, and used them to hang himself. He was found dead just after breakfast on Saturday morning."

"Oh, no. Poor boy." *And poor Nathan. No wonder he feels guilty!* "No wonder you despise Durham. His cruelty was responsible for another boy's death. Was he punished in any way?"

"The bagwig called him in for a talk, and afterward Durham and I met. Though he was older than I, we were much the same size, and I managed to give the bully a beating he did not soon forget. Unfortunately, it was a case of too little too late, and it did none of us any good. Young Partridge was still dead, and I was unable to put away my guilt at having turned a blind eye to his abuse."

Eugenia reached out and laid her hand upon Nathan's. "But you were just a boy."

"We were all boys! What has that to say to the situation? It did not absolve us from protecting someone who was unable to protect himself. We were not too young to learn what separates humans from the so-called lower animals.

"So many times in the years following Partridge's death I have asked myself who bears the greater guilt, the person who does the actual abusing, or the person who sees the wrong and merely walks by, telling himself he is minding his own business. I do not know the answer to that question, but I have come to believe that the safety of children—I should say, especially that of children—is the business of us all."

Chapter Ten

The servants at Swanleigh Hall had been notified that Mr. Seymour would arrive some time after the first of July, so they were prepared for his arrival. If the gentleman and his guest were less prepared for their reception, it was no wonder.

The coach turned off the lane, passed between two gray stone Doric columns that supported an arch of filigreed iron, and traversed the broad, straight carriageway to the front of the handsome gray stone house. The coachman had only just reined in the horses when the double ebony entrance doors were thrown open. A small procession composed of the butler, a young housemaid, and a plump, gray-haired lady who could only be the housekeeper hurried out, smiles of welcome upon their faces.

"Mr. Seymour," the butler greeted warmly when Nathan stepped from the coach. "We have missed you, sir."

"Thank you, Avery. I trust the cold that plagued you all winter has at last vanished."

"Without a trace, sir."

"And you, Mrs. Yardle," he greeted politely, as though it was the most natural occurrence in the world for his housekeeper to come out to meet his coach and bring with her one of the maids they occasionally hired from the village, "I hope I see you in good health as well."

The rosy-cheeked lady bobbed a curtsy and thanked him for his good wishes. "And I wish to thank you also, sir, for being so good as to escort my guest here for her visit with me. Miss Bailey did come with you, did she not?"

Nathan had only just reached his hand out to assist Eugenia from the carriage, and at the housekeeper's startling inquiry, he paused, exchanging confused stares with the young lady in question.

"Oh, there you are, Miss Bailey," the housekeeper said, coming forward, a smile upon her face. "I cannot tell you how pleased I was to get your note that you were to visit me at last. With Mr. Seymour's permission," she added, glancing at him as if waiting for some sign of approval, "I've prepared one of the guest suites, being as I've not got space enough to make you comfortable in my rooms."

Eugenia let Nathan assist her from the carriage, then she shook the housekeeper's outstretched hand. "How kind of you," she said, "I . . . er, hope it was no trouble."

"No trouble at all, my dear Miss Bailey. Now you come along with me, if you please. While Anna sees your things are taken up to your room, you and I will enjoy a cup of tea and a good coze. I want to hear all about the young ladies at your school."

Not at all certain what she should do, Eugenia looked at Nathan. Since his only response was a raised eyebrow, as if to say he was as perplexed as she, she gave in with as much grace as possible and allowed the housekeeper to link arms with her and take her into the Hall. Once they were inside the impressive vestibule with its gray-and-black Italian marble floor, the servant put her forefinger across her lips, signaling Eugenia to remain silent. "I will explain all when we are alone, miss."

Following the woman, Eugenia walked through the vestibule and to the left of a large room she assumed was the medieval banqueting hall from which the house got its name. They continued down a broad, bronze-and-green–carpeted corridor, past the kitchen, and into the housekeeper's rooms.

It was a pleasant apartment, with chintz-covered chairs drawn up to the fireplace, and close at hand stood a small mahogany Pembroke table whose leaves were in place and covered with a fresh linen cloth. A china teapot emitted a most heavenly aroma, and Eugenia found herself more than willing to remove her bonnet and pelisse, make herself comfortable in one of the chairs, and wait for Mrs. Yardle to pour her a cup of tea.

"And now," the servant said, handing Eugenia a cup of the well-steeped brew, "I can just imagine what you must be thinking, Miss Bailey, that you have landed among a gathering of Bedlamites."

When Eugenia would have denied any such thoughts, the housekeeper smiled to show she was speaking in jest. "I received a letter from Mr. Riddle," she said, "brought by that impudent little mudlark with the insatiable appetite."

It was Eugenia's turn to smile, for the woman could be referring to none other than Fiona, the little cockney maid. "How is she?"

"Saucy. Pert. Old beyond her years. Yet a likable lass for all her faults, and a willing worker, in spite of her habit of talking nineteen miles to the hour."

"I look forward to seeing her."

"And she you, miss. I've taken the liberty of putting a cot for her in the little dressing room off your bedchamber, since Fiona tells me that was the arrangement in town. But getting back to the letter; in it Mr. Riddle informed me that you were assisting the master with some project or other. He did not say what that might be exactly, but he took leave to sing your praises, Miss Bailey."

Though Eugenia felt warmth invade her cheeks, the housekeeper continued. "Mr. Riddle meant no impertinence by it, miss, but he wanted me and Mr. Avery to know that you were a real lady, and he asked that we do all within our power to shield you from the tongues of idle gossipers. With that in mind, me and Mr. Avery thought it would serve to stop any wagging tongues here in the village if I put it out that you were come to Swanleigh Hall to visit me. No need for a chaperone if you are my guest."

"But, I—"

"Anna," Mrs. Yardle added, "that's the maid I sent up to see to your things, lives in the village. If I know aught of the matter, by the time she returns to us on the morrow, there will not be a man, woman, or child in all of Stanton-on-Lee who does not know the name, approximate age, and occupation of my guest."

Quite overcome by such thoughtfulness, Eugenia said, "You are very kind, Mrs. Yardle."

"Not at all, miss. Fiona told us how you saved her from the brute who sold her into that unspeakable place—that den of iniquity—and it's happy we all are to have such a brave lady with us."

The housekeeper stood then, as if to indicate that the tea drinking was at an end and they were now on the footing of servant and guest of the master of the house. After bobbing a curtsy, she said, "I hope your stay will be enjoyable, Miss Bailey, and if there is aught I can do for you, you've but to let me know. Now, if you please, I will show you to your room."

Mrs. Yardle did not actually escort Eugenia herself, for rheumatism forced the woman to avoid the stairs as much as possible, but she called one of the kitchen maids to do the honors. The suite to which Eugenia was led was in the east wing, and the first thing she saw when she stepped into the pretty rose-and-cream bedchamber was Fiona, her blue eyes alight with pleasure.

"Well, Fiona," she said, pleased to see the child as well, "you look smart as five pence in your new uniform. And I believe you have filled out a bit since I saw you last. I suppose I need not ask if they are giving you enough to eat here at Swanleigh Hall."

"Coo ee, miss, you'll never believe the likes of the food they've got 'ere in the country. There's a poultry 'ouse fair filled to the rafters with fowls, and a garden just out the kitchen door where a body can pick vegetables right out of the ground. And there's even a concession 'ouse full of all sorts of fruits."

"Succession house," Eugenia said.

"And a lake," the young maid continued, her enthusiasm undaunted, "with swans floating all about. And you'll never guess, miss, but them swans—every bleedin' one of them—is black as pitch. They look like they've been painted they do. And they'll come right up to the shore and take food from a person's 'and."

Eugenia let the child talk on while she washed her face and hands and changed her clothes. She had worn her good olive green frock for traveling, but now she donned the plain, pale blue cambric that was the newest of her classroom dresses. It felt oddly liberating to wear her own clothes, and she descended the east wing staircase half an hour later, feeling happy to be in this lovely old house and even happier that she had not gone back to the school. Much better to be here . . . with Nathan. After all, the card party was but thirteen days away, and once that event came and went, she would return to the Misses Becknell for what might well be the remainder of her life.

Not that spending most of her adult life at the school was a new concept, for it was not. If in the past she had not been content with the prospect, at least she had been resigned to it. Now, however, the thought of returning there, and never seeing Nathan again, and Mr. Winfield, too, of course, left her feeling vaguely discontented.

I shall miss my new friends. I wish . . . No! She would not set herself up for disappointment. Only a fool wishes for things that can never happen.

Vowing to put all unproductive thoughts from her mind and to make the most of what promised to be a delightful sojourn, she continued down the stairs, where a footman waited to show her to Nathan's library. Once inside the room, she stopped to admire its decidedly masculine decor.

It was a much larger room than the library in town, with floor-to-ceiling bookshelves, and taking pride of place was a surprisingly well-preserved, antique Chinese desk. It was an unusual piece, embellished with a pair of carved dragons, and the red lacquered finish was beautifully complemented by an equally old red leather seaman's chest to the right of the unlit fireplace.

"Well," Nathan said, once the door was closed behind her, "I see you survived your welcome to Swanleigh Hall. Quite the drama, was it not? Unusual enough to enliven the arrival of even the most jaded traveler." With a sweep of his hand he invited her to be seated. "Did Mrs. Yardle explain about the letter from Riddle?"

"She did," Eugenia replied, disposing herself upon a wing chair upholstered in black and red stripes, "and I am touched by the thoughtfulness of your staff. They had no reason to wish me well, but they have, and I am most grateful. Now I can go about the countryside, visiting any place I wish, without needing to hide my identity."

"If that is the case," he said, "where would you like to venture first?"

"The hall, if you please, for I have never seen a real medieval banqueting hall."

"Nor will you now, I am afraid. My grandfather's father, in a moment of what could only be described as lunacy, had the room modernized."

"Oh, no. How . . . how unfortunate."

Nathan's tone was bland. "A tactful word, to be sure, but not one you would have used had you seen the results."

"Is it so bad?"

He shook his head. "Not now, for my father hired Robert Adam to do what he could to make amends. What we have is, I believe, a very handsome room, but aside from its residing in the center of the house, in the original space occupied by the hall, all other historical significance is now lost."

Having said this, he extended his hand to her, his manner easy, relaxed, as though they were friends of long standing. "Come. See for yourself."

Eugenia took his hand, and at the feel of his palm brushing against hers, warmth inched its way up her arm. After telling herself to ignore the sensation, she was thankful when Nathan released her so that she might precede him into the corridor. Her gratitude was short-lived, however, for as he led her to the vestibule—one of two entrances to the hall—he placed his hand at her back, and the feel of his strong fingers splayed against her spine sent shivers of delight throughout her entire body.

"This way," he said, obviously unaware of the effect his touch was having upon her, a circumstance for which Eugenia thanked heaven.

As she passed through the massive oak door, she breathed an "Oh," for the room was lovely.

Though she had hoped to see a true medieval hall complete with trestle tables, a dais for my lord and his exalted guests, and smoke screens at either end of the oblong room, she could find no fault with Robert Adam's finished product.

The hall had been reshaped into an octagon, a fact that was not evident from the corridor, and in each of the eight corners stood a twenty-foot green marble column. The domed roof was decorated in plaster scrolls finished in gold leaf, and upon each of the columns was one of the Muses, also layered in the thin gold.

Charmed by the statues, and happy for an excuse to move away from Nathan's disturbing presence, Eugenia circled the room, naming each of the sister goddesses of Greek mythology who presided over the various arts and sciences. "Where is the ninth Muse?" she asked. "Where is Terpsichore? Was there no room for the goddess of dance?"

Nathan leaned negligently against the doorjamb, watching her. A smile sat easily upon his handsome face, and his attitude was that of an amused host. "Madam, the room has but eight corners. Would you have Mr. Adam forsake artistic symmetry?"

"No, of course not."

"Besides," he continued, "if you recall, I have not neglected the lady entirely, for there is a marble sculpture of her in the drawing room in my town house."

"Yes. Now I think of it, I believe she stands in the niche to the left of the fireplace. Urania is there as well, is she not?" Not waiting for his reply, Eugenia returned to the column upon which the Muse of Astronomy stood, a globe of the world held aloft in her hand.

After giving a moment's study to the statue, Eugenia said, "I believe I prefer Urania as she appears in the marble. She seems more approachable without the elaborate gold adornment."

Prior to that moment, Nathan had not given the subject much thought, but now he nodded his agreement. He, too, preferred Urania in the polished stone. She seemed more natural, as if marble was her true element.

"She reminds me of you," he said.

He had not meant to say the words aloud. He had been recalling the first time he ever saw Eugenia—recalling how her smooth skin and her classical profile had brought to mind the simple lines of the marble goddess—and the words had just slipped out. Now, as he looked at the living, breathing woman before him, dressed in an unpretentious blue frock, her thick brown hair arranged neatly and without fuss, he decided he preferred Miss Eugenia Bailey as well without the fancy adornment.

No longer painted and dressed like some Cyprian, she appeared exactly what she was, a gently reared young lady who was modest, honest, and unbelievably lovely in her simplicity.

"I remind you of Urania?"

"Except for the eyes," he said, trying for a lighter tone. "In that instance, I do not prefer marble."

She grimaced. "You prefer the gold?"

"No," he said, "not at all. When it comes to eyes, I prefer them full of life, smiling and sincere." He looked directly at her; he could not stop himself. "And I like brown. Pure, warm brown."

"You do?" she asked softly, her gaze captured by his.

"Definitely."

While he spoke, he pushed away from the door, his posture no longer negligent, but purposeful as he moved toward her. He stopped just in front of her, his entire attention focused upon her face.

She looked up at him, and there was a question in her expression, as though she sought the answer to a riddle.

Nathan knew just how she felt, for he was attempting to solve a mystery of sorts himself. He had been acquainted with Eugenia Bailey for less than two weeks. When, in that brief period, had he stopped thinking of her as a plain schoolmistress and begun to think of her as a beautiful, desirable woman? A woman whose brown

eyes bid him get lost in their depths, while her tantaliz-
ing lips tempted him to explore their softness.

He was within arm's reach of her when a discreet
cough from just behind him put an end to whatever he
had been about to say, or do, and Nathan stopped, not
certain if he was pleased or disappointed by the inter-
ruption.

"Your pardon, sir," the butler said. "The cold collation
you requested is ready, and I have taken it to the library."

"Excellent. Thank you, Avery."

As though it had been his original reason for approaching her, Nathan took Eugenia's elbow and turned
her toward the door. "Come," he said, "let us have something to eat. Then if you think you would enjoy it, I
should like to show you the swans for which the Hall
was named."

After a delicious nuncheon of shaved ham and crusty
rolls, followed by a bowl of fresh strawberries with
cream, Eugenia returned to her bedchamber for her
walking boots. Though the day was sunny and bright, a
breeze played among the trees, so she donned the Prussian blue spencer and a silk bonnet for their walk to the
lake.

Appropriately attired, she joined Nathan once again in
the library, and together they exited the book room by
way of the French windows that opened onto a small
side garden bordered by a thick row of old rose bushes.
The delicate perfume of the pale pink roses filled the air,
and even after Nathan and Eugenia had crunched their
way down a crushed-stone footpath that led around to
the rear of the house, she fancied she could still smell the
wonderful aroma of the flowers.

Though the lake was visible from the Hall, it was perhaps three-quarters of a mile away, and it lay at the bottom of a gently rolling hill. The vista resembled a

landscape painting in green and blue—green grass, blue sky, and even bluer water—and upon the hill, a dozen or so brown-and-white Ayrshire milk cows stood about munching grass while their calves frolicked nearby. As for the famous swans, at that distance they were not visible.

"Careful where you step," Nathan warned, putting his hand beneath her elbow. "The countryside is pocked with rabbit holes just waiting to trip the unwary. I should hate to see you fall."

They walked in silence until they reached the bottom of the hill, where they stopped, as if by prearrangement, to gaze across the calm surface of the water. At the shore's edge, slender willow trees trailed the tips of their lacy green branches into the cool liquid as if refreshing themselves; while in the middle of the lake, a flock of graceful blue-black swans glided slowly, effortlessly, leaving the merest trace of a ripple in their wake.

"What do you think of it?" Nathan asked quietly.

Surprised by the question, she said, "I think what everyone who sees it must think."

"But I am not interested in what everyone else thinks. It is your opinion I sought, Eugenia. Your impression I wished to hear."

"It is lovely," she said, somewhat breathlessly, for she had to wonder why he had expressed himself with such particularity. She could not help but be confused, for Nathan seemed almost to be singling her out. And yet, how was she to judge such matters when she knew so little of the world—knew so little of the kind of behavior deemed acceptable in sophisticated men of the world?

Earlier, when they had stood before the statues of the Muses, Eugenia could have sworn Nathan was about to kiss her. He had crossed the room, his movement purposeful, his gaze intent, and when he stopped but inches away from her, she felt herself practically drowning in his unfathomable gray eyes. Her heart began to pound and her knees seemed almost too weak to sustain her. In another moment she would have been obliged to lean against him for support.

Then the butler had coughed, and Nathan had taken her arm as though that had been his intention all along. Eugenia had not known what to think. Had she imagined it all? She felt confused, out of her depth.

Now here he was asking her opinion of his home as if her answer were of importance to him. Almost as if he wished to . . .

No! I will not delude myself! I will not be one of those pitiful females who sees a gentleman smile and imagines it is a declaration of love. Nor will I take a simple question and read into it a desire on the questioner's part to make me an offer of his hand, to make me mistress of his home.

With any other gentleman, and in any other place, Eugenia might have allowed herself to think the man felt his home was in need of a woman's touch. As it happened, nothing could have been further from the truth, for Swanleigh Hall was beautifully appointed, smoothly run, and eminently comfortable.

"It is lovely," she repeated, "the Hall, the estate, the lake. I can understand why you were eager to return to it. London cannot compare with such a home, or with such magnificent scenery."

"So," said a voice from behind them, "this is a fine thing, I must say."

They both turned to discover Mr. Martin Winfield striding toward them, his face a study in feigned anger. "I cannot credit that you would treat a friend with such callous disregard, Nate, especially when you knew Miss Eugenia had promised to allow *me* to show her the swans. I see I shall be obliged to call you out."

Nathan made his friend a mock bow and stepped

aside, as if surrendering his rights as escort. "I beg your pardon, Winny."

"As well you might, old boy."

The newcomer approached Eugenia and bowed over her hand. "Good afternoon, ma'am. Do I find you suitably impressed by the splendor of the lake and the black swans?"

Eugenia returned his smile, more happy than she could say at his timely arrival, for with him she knew exactly where she stood. She liked Winny, and he liked her; their friendship was uncomplicated. She could relax with this pleasant gentleman, for she never experienced any of the bewildering emotions she felt when in company with Nathan Seymour. "Yes to both your questions, sir. The lake is splendid, and no one could fail to be impressed by such beautiful beasts. They are so majestic. One might liken them to harmony in motion."

"Harmony? If you can use that word, ma'am, I must suppose you have not heard them speak."

"I have not, sir. Is it so bad?"

"Bad?" He rolled his eyes heavenward. "The word does not begin to describe their infernal *maul maul*. The noise is discordant in the extreme. Only let them see a hawk or some other large bird in the sky, and they will set up such a racket that I defy you to hear it without resorting to covering your ears."

"Winny," Nathan said, breaking in upon his friend's nonsense. "You arrived in good time. I assume you got my note?"

"I did, old boy. And none too soon, I might add, for the landlord dropped me a not very subtle hint yesterday that I should pay a little something on my back rent. The fellow had the effrontery to inform me there was another gentleman who was interested in having my rooms."

Eugenia must have shown her surprise at being privy to such a conversation, for Mr. Winfield offered her his apology. "I quite forgot myself. The thing is, ma'am, I have come to think of you as one of us, and I feel so comfortable with you that I speak freely, as one does before a friend. Pray, accept my apology if I have given offense."

"On the contrary, Mr. Winfield. Far from being offended, I am honored to be numbered among your friends."

"No, no," he said, his countenance beet red with embarrassment, "the honor is all mine. Word of a gentleman."

As if to put an end to the conversation, the red-faced gentleman offered her his arm and asked if he might escort her to the water's edge for a closer look at the ebony fowl. When she agreed, he looked pointedly at Nathan. "Fair's fair, old boy. Miss Eugenia has made her choice. You may run along now."

"I think not," Nathan said, giving the smaller man a mocking look. "I believe I will accompany you and the lady, for I am experiencing an almost overwhelming desire to discover how the swans will react when I toss you into the lake. It should be interesting to see just how harmonious *your* squawking will be."

"Ignore him," Winny said. "The poor fellow was always jealous of me."

Nathan's rejoinder, whatever it may have been, was muffled by a sudden and very loud clap of thunder, and within minutes raindrops began to spatter the heads and shoulders of the trio of bird fanciers. In complete agreement at last, all three abandoned further investigation of the fowl in favor of a judicious run for cover, with each gentleman holding one of Eugenia's hands to assist her to greater speed up the hill.

Unfortunately, they were not fast enough. By the time they reached the crushed-stone footpath that led to the library, the rain was coming down in earnest and had soaked right through the thin muslin of Eugenia's dress, leaving her sodden from head to toe and shivering with the cold.

"Ring for Avery," Nathan said the moment the French windows were closed behind them. "Tell him to send a maid and lots of hot water to Eugenia's bedchamber. She is chilled through to the bone, and I want her made warm as quickly as possible. Half the staff came down with the influenza this past winter, and I want no recurrences."

While Winny crossed the room to summon the servant, Nathan raised the lid of the red leather seaman's chest, removed a brightly colored afghan, and shook the knitted wool throw free of its folds. Without asking Eugenia's permission, he draped the afghan over her back then brought the ends around and knotted them across her chest. When the cover was secured, he drew the shivering lady into his arms to share with her whatever warmth remained in his body.

Eugenia was much too cold to refuse the slightly musty-smelling afghan. As for being held against Nathan's broad chest, his arms wrapped about her, she had not the least desire to reject that source of warmth— far from it. She was so accepting of this unexpected solicitousness on the gentleman's part that she nestled her forehead against the strong column of his throat, breathing deeply of the clean, masculine smell of his skin.

When he pulled her even closer, all thought of rain and cold vanished from Eugenia's consciousness. She was aware of nothing but the strength of Nathan's arms, the hard, lean length of his body, and the magical heat that enveloped her.

The instant the butler answered the bell, Winny gave the instructions regarding the maid and the hot water.

"And send up a glass of brandy," Nathan added.

Before Eugenia knew what was happening, Nathan had swooped her up into his arms, blanket and all. He carried her down the corridor and up the staircase that led to her suite, and not once did she protest the cavalier treatment. Instead, she laid her head against his shoulder, closed her eyes, and gave herself up to the wonder of being in his arms, cared for and protected.

Chapter Eleven

The next few days were the happiest of Eugenia's adult life. She suffered no ill effects from being drenched by the cold rain, thanks in part to having soaked in a tub of steaming water, then consuming a bowl of sustaining beef broth and sleeping for at least ten undisturbed hours that night.

If she awoke the next morning to the memory of being held in Nathan's arms, and with a feeling of well-being she had not experienced since she was a child, she was not surprised, for just before she drifted into those hours of repose, she had admitted to herself something she had been refusing to acknowledge for the past week. She admitted she was in love with Nathan Seymour.

It was crazy. It was foolish beyond permission. But it was a fact she would no longer deny. She loved Nathan, and she would love him for the rest of her life.

She did not expect him to return her feelings; after all, he was a man accustomed to beautiful, sophisticated women, and as Henrietta Parker had told her, even the most beautiful of Nathan's flirts and mistresses began to bore him after a few weeks. Eugenia understood this, and unlike those foolish women who had thought they could charm him into falling in love with them, she suffered from no such delusions.

She did not aspire to becoming Mrs. Nathan Seymour.

Always a practical person, Eugenia would not let herself dream of such an eventuality, for at the end of that foolish fantasy waited a broken heart. But even sensible females sometimes fell in love with scoundrels. Knowing there was no hope for a future with the man she loved, she gave her heart permission to enjoy the twelve days that remained until the card party.

She would not become Nathan's mistress—even if he should ask it of her; she would not forsake her own principles in deference to his—but she meant to savor each moment spent in his company. Too soon she would be back at school, with the weeks turning into years, and if the next twelve days were all she would ever spend with the man who had stolen her heart, she vowed not to waste a moment in wishful thinking.

Carpe diem was her new philosophy. She would seize the day, beginning with that moment.

After drinking every last drop of the bubbly hot chocolate Fiona brought her, and eating every morsel of the currant bun, she informed the young maid that she meant to dress for church.

"The guv wants you to stay abed, miss. 'E told me not to—"

"Mr. Seymour is your employer, Fiona, and you are obliged to obey his orders. He does not employ me, however, so I am at liberty to do exactly as I see fit."

After throwing back the covers, Eugenia padded barefoot across the pretty rose-patterned carpet and opened the chiffonnier. "I appreciate everyone's concern for my health, but after a good night's rest, I am quite my old self again and perfectly able to attend services. If the gentlemen do not mean to attend, would you ask Mrs. Yardle if I might accompany her?"

While Fiona went belowstairs to deliver the message to the housekeeper, Eugenia donned her olive green muslin and a chip straw bonnet. When she arrived in the vestibule some twenty minutes later, she found the house-keeper and both the gentlemen waiting for her.

After an exchange of greetings all around, and an inquiry from Mr. Winfield regarding her health, Eugenia allowed Nathan to assist her into the landau, where she took her place beside Mrs. Yardle in the forward-facing seat. They arrived in Stanton-on-Lee with but a few minutes to spare, but even if they had not been among the last of the worshipers to arrive at the small, fourteenth-century stone church, their arrival would have occasioned remark.

Familiar with the inquisitiveness of villagers, Eugenia knew there would be a few whispers when the foursome entered the sanctuary, and she was not the least surprised that those whispers grew more excited as the Swanleigh Hall housekeeper and her guest were ushered into the family pew. If Eugenia was any judge of the matter, this show of condescension on the part of the wealthiest man in the neighborhood would be the main topic of conversation for weeks to come.

"Do not be overset," Mrs. Yardle whispered once they were seated. "The villagers may be a mite nosy, but they're a good-hearted lot for all that."

The truth of the housekeeper's statement was evident after the service when dozens of the villagers stopped by to be introduced to Mrs. Yardle's guest, each of them bidding her welcome. It was while Eugenia conversed with the baker's wife about the many peace celebrations taking place in London that a young lady of perhaps twenty summers caught her attention. The damsel, a diminutive blonde with a sweet countenance and wide blue eyes, stood politely a few feet away, but when Eugenia chanced to smile at her, she approached shyly.

"Miss Bailey?" she said.

"Yes?"

"I cannot hope that you will remember me, ma'am, but

I was at the Misses Becknell's Academy when you first came there as an assistant teacher. My name is Dora Trillin."

"Of course," Eugenia said, taking the proffered hand in hers. "I remember you quite well, Miss Trillin, for yours were the neatest embroidery stitches I have ever seen."

The young lady blushed prettily. "I saw you when you first arrived this morning, Miss Bailey, and I thought . . . that is, I hoped . . . we might have an opportunity to renew our acquaintance."

"I should like that very much."

"It was during the final hymn that I remembered how interested you always were in history, and I wondered if you were staying in the neighborhood long enough for me to show you Verulamium, the Roman ruins? That is," she continued shyly, "if Mrs. Yardle can spare you for an afternoon."

The housekeeper heard this last and turned from her own conversation with the blacksmith's wife. Dropping the young lady a curtsy, she said, "Good day to you, Miss Trillin. I hope Lady Trillin is enjoying good health. And Sir James?"

"Yes, thank you. My parents are well. Mother and Father are just over there with the vicar."

The young lady blushed again, obviously not knowing what protocol ruled in such cases as this, when someone she wished to introduce to her mother was visiting a servant in another house. Fortunately, Nathan solved the problem by stepping forward and making the young lady a bow.

"Miss Trillin, is it not?" he said, employing a smile guaranteed to melt the heart of any female between the ages of nine and ninety. "Did I hear you say, ma'am, that you wished to kidnap one of Swanleigh Hall's guests?"

"Yes, sir. If I may. Miss Bailey was a favorite with all the girls at the academy, myself included. I cannot tell you how delighted I was to see her again after all these years."

"It cannot be so very many years," he said, his tone a fine blend of mockery and gallantry, "for I seem to recall when Sir James set you on your first pony. A Shetland, I believe it was."

"Yes, sir. It . . . it was a Shetland."

"Bad form, Nate, old boy," Martin Winfield interrupted, stepping forward to join the group. "Mustn't recall such things about a lady. Next you will be telling us how she fell off the pony and skinned her knees."

"Oh, no. He could not," the lady in question replied softly, turning the full force of her blue orbs upon the newly arrived gentleman, "for Gallant Bess was the sweetest pony who ever lived. She is with us still, for I could not bring myself to part with her."

Mr. Winfield, already intrigued by the rare occurrence of encountering a female who was short enough to be obliged to look up at him, appeared quite stunned by those wide, guileless eyes. Turning to Eugenia, he said, "If you would be so kind, Miss Eugenia, would you make me known to your friend?"

She had no more than finished the introductions when Mr. Winfield was struck with what he called a capital idea. "I heard you mention the Roman ruins, Miss Trillin. I have been longing this age to view them. What think you of my accompanying you and Miss Eugenia on your ride?"

If Nathan was surprised to discover that his old school chum harbored a desire to see the ruins, it was not to be wondered at, especially since he had suggested such an expedition at least a dozen times on Winny's previous visits to Swanleigh Hall. On each of those occasions, he had received the rather rude reply that his guest had no time for "some fusty old relics." Remembering his friend's words, Nathan could only assume that Winny's

sudden interest in antiquities was due solely to the chit
with the big blue eyes.

Turning to Eugenia, Nathan asked, "Do you ride,
madam?"

"I was used to, sir. Though it has been several years
since the opportunity came my way."

"A bit rusty, are you?"

She smothered a chuckle. "I refuse to admit to anything so *outre*! And I must tell you, sir, that I find it un-
gallant of you to liken me to a piece of tinware ready for
the dust bin."

Eugenia knew he was teasing her, and she had a pretty
fair notion what he had in mind. "I do admit, however, to
being a bit out of practice. Therefore, if you are afraid to
trust me with one of your horses, sir, perhaps it is as well
that Mr. Winfield accompany us, to ensure that I and the
mount return in one piece."

Nathan appeared to ponder the plan. "I cannot think
that an altogether practical scheme, Miss Bailey, and I
marvel at your falling in with it, you being an educator of
the young. Reason must tell you that if Winny is obliged
to keep an eye on two ladies at once, he cannot possibly
appreciate the wonders of the ruins."

With a dramatic sigh, Eugenia said, "I fear you are in
the right of it, sir. It was selfish of me not to consider Mr.
Winfield's feelings. Perhaps the expedition is not such a
good idea after all. Had we better cancel it, do you
think?"

"No!" Mr. Winfield said. "What I mean is, no need to
cancel on my account. No need at all. I am certain we can
solve this dilemma." He gave it a moment's thought. "I
have it. If you are fearful for your cattle, Nate, why not
come with us?"

"Yes. Please do," Miss Trillin said. "We should be delighted to have you."

"A good idea, actually," Mr. Winfield continued. "Glad

I thought of it. We could make a party of it. Take a picnic basket, that sort of thing. Besides, Miss Trillin's parents know you and will be more likely to agree to the scheme if you are with us."

"Hmm," Nathan said. "You are right, Winny. Perhaps I should come along as well, to ensure that no harm befalls a guest under my roof."

Aware of his status as the owner of the largest estate in the neighborhood, and knowing the answer to his question even before he asked it, he bowed to the young lady. "What say you, Miss Trillin? Shall I ask Sir James to have the Shetland saddled?"

The young lady blushed hotly, but she nodded her consent, obviously as aware as Nathan that her parents would never refuse an invitation issued by the owner of Swanleigh Hall.

The matter settled to everyone's satisfaction, Dora Trillin linked arms with her former teacher and took her over to meet her parents. Since the gentlemen followed close behind them, Sir James and Lady Trillin greeted them all with unallayed pleasure.

Within a matter of minutes, the excursion to the ancient Roman city of Verulamium was set for the following day. Lady Trillin was beside herself with excitement, and she extended an invitation for the riding party to stop in for tea following the outing. If she found anything to dislike in the idea of entertaining a guest of the Swanleigh Hall housekeeper, she kept the fact to herself.

"We will come for you about ten," Nathan informed the young lady. "If that time is satisfactory."

"Of course it is," replied her mama, looking as pleased as the cat who fell into the cream pot. "She will be ready, Mr. Seymour. Our little Dora is always so very punctual. Is she not, Sir James?"

"Yes, yes. As you say, m'dear. Always punctual."

"A quality of inestimable value," Nathan said, bowing over Lady Trillin's hand. "Until tomorrow, ma'am."

"Until tomorrow," her ladyship repeated. She was still waving her handkerchief and smiling when the landau containing Nathan and his party turned from the church yard into the lane.

"Oh, Sir James," she said, once the carriage was out of sight. "Only think of it. Our Dora and Mr. Seymour."

"I don't think of it," replied her husband. "The man's too jaded by half. And much too old for our girl."

"What foolishness," replied his wife. "A wealthy gentleman is never too old, and I mean to have him for our Dora."

"Happen you'll catch cold on that, m'dear. Females have been trying to snag Nathan Seymour this age and more. Much better to concentrate on young Winfield. Good family there. I was at Eton with his father. Besides, I suspect Seymour has his eye on Mrs. Yardle's young friend."

"The schoolteacher? Do not be ridiculous."

"Not ridiculous at all. A pretty-behaved young woman, and she looked to have a deal more sense than most."

"Men," his wife said, rolling her eyes heavenward, as if asking for patience. "She may be pretty behaved, as you say, but the woman is six-and-twenty if she is a day. Quite at her last prayers, as the saying goes. And her frock. Why, if I know anything of the matter, it was made by some village seamstress."

"And what has that to say to anything?"

"Only that Seymour may have a reputation as a scoundrel, but he knows what is due to his family. When it comes time to marry, depend upon it, he will choose a lady worthy of his name, and not some nobody without a penny to bless herself with."

"Coming it a bit strong, m'dear. I thought her rather taking."

"Of course *you* did. You are a middle-aged man who resides in the country twelve months out of the year, and you have not Seymour's discriminating taste. As for him having his eye on Miss Bailey, you may trust me when I tell you that he was merely being polite to her. I should be surprised to discover that he utters more than half a dozen words to her between now and tomorrow's excursion."

Nathan's supposed politeness more than exceeded those half dozen words. In fact, it continued throughout the nuncheon served them upon their return from the village, and Lady Trillin might have been surprised to know what a merry trio the two gentlemen and the lady at her last prayers made, talking and laughing like old friends.

After the meal, Nathan's chivalry was still not exhausted, and he took Eugenia down to the stables so she might choose her own mount. As they strolled across the freshly swept brick floor toward the far end where the saddle horses were stalled, he asked, "Approximately how long has it been since you rode?"

"Seven years."

"A long time, surely, but you are an intelligent woman. If you feel confident in your ability, I trust your judgment."

She gave him a saucy look. "Do not, I beg of you, try to turn me up sweet. 'Tis a waste of time, sir, for the word 'rusty' is still sounding in my ears. Did you think I would forget so soon?"

He chuckled. "That rankled, did it?"

"Oh, no. Not at all. As you say, I am an intelligent woman, and as such, I make allowances for the ragtag manners of gentlemen who have been kowtowed to all their lives simply because of their wealth and standing in society."

"A flush hit!" he said, placing his hand over his heart as if wounded.

They had arrived at the next-to-last stall, where a bay gelding perhaps sixteen hands high whickered and lifted his massive head, as if in greeting. "Hello," Nathan said, running his hand down the animal's neck. "How are you, Sheik, old fellow?"

When the gelding saw Eugenia, he straightened, his ears back, as if to protest the presence of a stranger, but he settled down quickly when Nathan produced a small apple from inside his pocket and held it balanced on his palm, his fingers flat. Like a well-mannered guest at a tea party, Sheik stretched forward and gently took the fruit between his yellowed incisors. Nathan and Eugenia left him noisily grinding the treat between his powerful molars.

At the last stall, a pretty little gray mare came forward at sight of the visitors and stretched her head beyond the stall door as if happy to greet them, strangers or not. Eugenia was charmed by the animal's gentle manners and reached forward to stroke the velvety nose. "Hello, you pretty creature," she said.

When the mare nuzzled Eugenia's hand, inviting more attention, Eugenia obliged by stroking the animal's forehead. "You are a sweet thing. And you act with far more refinement than that big fellow over there."

"Now you have wounded me," Nathan said, "for I thought I was acting with a marked degree of refinement."

Eugenia turned quickly, her lips pressed together to keep them from smiling. "I did not mean you, sir. Though now I think on it—"

"Spare me," he said. "I am fast coming to the conclusion that educated women think far too much. It can put a man off his feed."

"Oh? And am I to conclude from that observation, sir, that you do not approve of educated women?"

"Me?" he asked, his gray eyes filled with a teasing light, "not a bit of it." He fetched another small apple from his pocket, then bit into the fruit and began to chew it, all the while holding Eugenia's gaze with his. "As you see, madam, my appetite is just fine."

A drop of apple juice lingered on his top lip, and while Eugenia watched, Nathan used the tip of his tongue to capture the nectar. "Umm," he said, still looking at her, "delicious."

Already relaxed by his teasing manner, Eugenia found herself mesmerized by the sight of his tongue searching out the juice on his lip. Without realizing she did so, she moistened her own lips. Though unconsciously done, her action had an immediate effect upon Nathan, for he raised one questioning eyebrow, then still holding her gaze, he walked slowly toward her.

The breath seemed to catch in Eugenia's throat, and as Nathan came closer, his steps deliberate, his movement lithe and almost predatory, she felt a tingling awareness begin somewhere deep within, a tingling that slowly radiated to every part of her body. When he was but inches away, he put his free hand upon the stall post just behind her, leaning close and effectively blocking her from escape. Not that she had any thought of trying to flee.

When she did not bid him move away, he brought the apple close to her mouth. "Would you like a taste?" he asked, the words low and soft.

Eugenia's heart began to race, and though she had never cared much for apples, she took a bite.

Nathan watched her while she chewed and swallowed, then he bent his head, bringing his mouth just a soft breath away from hers. "Now," he said, his voice husky, "*I* want a taste."

His lips touched hers. Lightly. Gently. Lingering only

a moment. "Very delicious," he whispered, then licked his lips again, as if savoring the sweetness.

Eugenia watched his every move, not even daring to breathe for fear he would not want another taste. Her thoughts must have shown upon her face, for he touched his mouth to hers once again. This time, his lips lingered, then brushed lightly back and forth against hers, setting Eugenia's entire being on fire and making her think she might faint from the wonder of Nathan kissing her.

Her knees seemed to grow weak, and as she placed her hand upon Nathan's chest to keep from falling, she heard a loud chomp startlingly close to her ear. Unable to stop herself, she cried out.

"What the devil!" Nathan said. Almost as startled as Eugenia, he straightened, then looked at his right hand, the one that had once held the half-eaten apple. While he examined his fingers for teeth marks, Eugenia turned toward the little mare, who was placidly grinding the last of the apple between her molars.

Before she could stop herself, Eugenia chuckled.

For a moment, Nathan stared at her, unable to credit that she was laughing. Within seconds, however, the humor of the situation overcame his surprise that a woman he had just kissed was not swooning in his arms, and he found himself laughing as well.

"Madam, I thought you said that animal's manners were refined."

"They are," Eugenia replied, trying not to laugh again. "How can you even question the fact? After all, before she claimed the apple, she let you and me take the first bites."

Chapter Twelve

Monday dawned clear and warm, with a sky so blue it seemed to reach to eternity, and as the foursome rode down the narrow lane that led to the Roman ruins, a gentle breeze brought the subtle fragrance of late-blooming rhododendron. Here and there along the lane clusters of the tall, thick bushes appeared, some sporting bright orange blossoms, others adorned with dark pink.

Mr. Winfield and Dora Trillin, a surprisingly accomplished horsewoman, led the way, often breaking into a gallop for a short distance, with Eugenia and Nathan following at a somewhat slower pace. The trip took little more than an hour, but by the time they reached the remains of the ancient city of Verulamium, Eugenia's muscles were crying out for respite. The little mare had proved a sweet goer, with a soft mouth and a willingness to please; even so, Eugenia was delighted when Nathan dismounted and came around to help her down.

He put his hands on either side of her waist and lifted her from the saddle in a most gentlemanly manner, but when she looked into his eyes and saw the unholy light there, she pushed him away. "Do not say it," she commanded.

"Madam," he replied, "the word 'rusty' never entered my mind. Except, of course, when I first beheld you in this very fetching habit. What would *you* call the . . . uh, reddish color?"

"Copper," she said emphatically.

"Ah, yes. Copper."

Nathan looked her over, much as he had done when she first appeared in the vestibule earlier that morning. He had never seen her look so beautiful. The warm, coppery hue of the poplin jacket and skirt perfectly suited her satiny complexion, and the snuff brown hat with its copper-colored feather was a perfect foil for her lively brown eyes. "Whatever the color," he said, "you look charming."

At the simple compliment, the stiffness in Eugenia's muscles seemed to melt away. She had not meant to bring any of the clothes she had from Henrietta Parker, but somehow the habit had found its way into her trunk. Except for the color, it was a modest ensemble, and when she saw the way Nathan looked at her, his eyes telling her that he found her attractive, Eugenia was happy the habit had been packed.

She had spent most of last night lying in her bed, reliving that quarter hour in the stable—reliving those kisses and feeling anew the magic of Nathan's lips upon hers. Even as she thrilled at the memory, she could not stop the doubts that crept into her thoughts. When next they met, she wondered, would Nathan treat her with studied politeness, acting as if nothing had happened between them? Would he regret having kissed her? Would he wish he could send her back to London so he need not look at her again?

Obviously, the answer to all her questions was no, for as they prepared to leave Swanleigh Hall, just before Nathan tossed her into the saddle, he had leaned forward and spoken close to her ear, so only she could hear. "I wish I had an apple," he said.

At his teasing words, all the doubts of the night before

had vanished, and though Eugenia knew their kisses would never mean to Nathan what they had meant to her, at least he did not regret them.

"Miss Bailey," Dora Trillin called, breaking into Eugenia's thoughts, "the ruins are just the other side of that hill. What say you, shall we see them now or wait until after we eat?"

Nathan had sent a maid and a footman ahead in a farm wagon, and the pair were at that moment setting up the picnic just at the top of the hill. They had chosen a delightful spot near a stand of beech trees whose light green canopy would provide shade later in the day.

"I am destined to march up and down hills," Eugenia said beneath her breath.

"But this time," Nathan said, surprising her in that he was close enough to hear the remark, "there is not a cloud in the sky. I promise that you may safely traverse this hill without risking another soaking.

"Furthermore," he added, taking her hand and placing it in the crook of his arm, "if we walk slowly, no one need ever know that the ride was too much for a lady of your advanced age."

Eugenia gave him a quelling look before raising her voice to call to the young lady. "If you and Winny do not mind delaying the picnic, Dora, I believe a nice walk is just what I need."

"Capital idea," Mr. Winfield replied, finding nothing to dislike in the scheme. After asking something of Dora that made her laugh, he and the much younger lady raced one another up the hill, laughing most of the way. They stopped when they came to the stand of beeches, where they turned to wait for Nathan and Eugenia, who followed at a more sedate pace.

"Miss Bailey," Dora called out to her. "Before we crest the hill, I should like to ask you to close your eyes."

"Close my eyes? But I do not—"

"Please, ma'am."

"Do as she asks," Nathan said quietly. "I promise you, you will not regret it, for the city is more spectacular if it is viewed in one grand panorama."

Though Eugenia thought such instructions a bit on the dramatic side, she did as she was bid; not for anything would she forgo seeing the Roman city at its best. With her arm still in Nathan's, she let him lead her to the top of the hill, and when they stopped, she waited quietly until someone told her she might look.

"Now," Dora said, her voice suitably hushed. "Welcome to Verulamium."

When Eugenia opened her eyes, the sight before her fairly took her breath away. "Oh," she said, the word a mere whisper. "Oh, my."

Dora had been wise to bring them to this spot; from this elevated vantage point it was possible to see how the city had been laid out from one end to the other, using the rectangular Roman street patterns. Though time and weather had taken their toll upon the ancient remains, if a person stayed very still and concentrated only on the fine stretch of city wall that stood intact, and the Roman theater with its colonnaded stage, it was possible to imagine the area as it must have looked during the time of Christ.

The effect was almost mystical.

Even at a distance, it was possible to detect small stretches of the original Roman roads, though the pavement appeared overgrown with grasses. As well, here and there fragments of fallen columns lay upon the ground, their once beautiful shapes all but hidden by vivid yellow creeping buttercup intermingled with clumps of white campion.

Eugenia could not imagine anything more exciting than the spectacle before her, but Nathan soon showed her how mistaken one could be.

"If you will look farther," he said, pointing to an expanse of ground above and behind the remains of Verulamium, "you will see the banks and ditches of an Iron Age settlement, a prehistoric sight that must have inspired awe even in the Romans."

Eugenia, too, was awed.

Thankfully, no one saw fit to chatter, and she was allowed to look her fill in silence. The only sound was the rich, clear song of a skylark soaring aloft, but the beautiful song only added to Eugenia's enjoyment. In keeping with the wonder of the moment, she could easily imagine that a similar little bird had soared and sung in just such a manner when helmeted centurions trod the streets below.

Finally, when she could absorb no more, Eugenia sighed. "How marvelous," she said. "Thank you both for bringing me here. You could not have given me a finer gift. I shall treasure it forever."

For just a moment, Nathan stared at her, unable to believe that any female had uttered such words; however, the wonder he saw in her eyes obliged him to suspend his incredulity. She had spoken in earnest. To Eugenia Bailey, this was a gift worthy of praise.

Unbidden, the memory of a quite different sort of present invaded Nathan's thoughts. It was the evening of the masked ball, and he recalled the look on Eugenia's face when she had opened the black leather jeweler's box and found the gold filigree necklace with the diamond pendant. Nathan had expected her to be thrilled, and when she had looked more embarrassed than pleased, he had not known what to think. Later, of course, when he got to know her a little better, he realized the jewelry was not at all suitable for her. It was too gaudy, too showy, the kind of glittery geegaw a man gave his *chere amie*.

"I knew you would like it, Miss Bailey." Dora Trillin's words brought Nathan's thoughts back to the moment.

"You always had an appreciation for those things that truly matter."

Once again, Nathan was caught off guard. How had this young girl—this chit with little or no experience of the world—seen the real Eugenia when he had not? The question had no answer, but merely led to another question: When had Nathan become so jaded he could no longer tell the difference between a female whose only object was money, and a genuine lady?

He was disturbed by the questions, and not a little dismayed by the realization that he might have become the kind of scoundrel most of society already believed him to be. Eugenia Bailey had come to him for help in recovering money from Lord Durham, and the only idea that had presented itself to Nathan was to turn a decent woman into a make-believe lightskirt. Was this the act of a gentleman?

Every day, every hour that Eugenia spent in his company, her reputation, her very livelihood were at risk; yet Nathan had done little to protect her from discovery. From the moment he had heard her plan, his main objective had been to wreak havoc upon Cedric Durham, the man he despised, and he had not really thought of the long-term consequences Eugenia might suffer if any part of the plan went awry.

Thankfully, his unflattering recollections were cut short by the lady herself. He felt her hand upon his arm, and when he looked at her, she was smiling. "I am ready for the picnic."

"Found your appetite, have you?"

"Yes," she said. "Let the Italians say, 'See Rome and die.' I say, see Verulamium and eat."

He laughed. "Better not let Miss Trillin hear you say that. It would disappoint her to discover that the paragon she so admires is, in fact, a hedonistic Philistine."

"Not a hedonistic one," Eugenia corrected, "merely a hungry one."

The day that started with such promise did not disappoint; in fact, it seemed to get better with each hour. Eugenia had been enchanted by her initial view of the Roman ruins, and after a delicious meal, Nathan escorted her down the hill for a closer look.

They strolled about the ancient city for perhaps two hours, exploring every paving stone, investigating every column, and during that time Eugenia could not have asked for a more attentive escort or a more enjoyable companion. If her heart skipped a beat each time Nathan smiled at her, or her senses came alive each time he took her hand, those were just little added treats to make a wonderful day perfect.

Too soon it was time to go, and after Nathan tossed her into the saddle, he set a pace that made as little demand as possible upon her sore muscles. Once again Dora and Winny led the way, and only when they entered the gates at Trillin Manor did they pause to wait for Nathan and Eugenia.

Lady Trillin had outdone herself over the tea, serving dainty sandwiches, jam and bread, macaroons, three types of cake, and a tray of comfits. Though her attention to Nathan's every need was effusive, he bore it with a politeness that did him credit, and in doing so, he allowed Winny an extra hour spent in Dora's company.

After the refreshments had been devoured, and the guests had expressed their appreciation for the hospitality, they bid farewell to Sir James, Lady Trillin, and Dora, and were at last free to go.

It had been a delightful day, and for Eugenia, the return to Swanleigh Hall did not put an end to the experience. When Nathan assisted her from the saddle, a smile played upon his lips, a smile that told her without words that he, too, had enjoyed their time together.

"Thank you," Eugenia said, "for showing me some of the wonders of Hertfordshire."

"No," Nathan corrected, "it is I who should thank you, for allowing me to see these wonders through your eyes. I had almost forgotten why I love this land."

Having said this, he took her hand and escorted her down the east wing corridor and to the bottom of the stairs. "And now," he said, "if I am to show you more of the beauties of the county, you must attend to those over-worked muscles."

He insisted that she soak in a tub of steaming water, and after the leisurely bath, she felt immensely better. Though still slightly damp, she donned a fresh wrapper and freed her hair, combing her fingers through the strands so they fell about her back and shoulders; then she stretched out on the day bed for a much needed rest.

Almost immediately, sleep tried to claim her, but Eugenia would not succumb. She did not want to surrender the ephemeral cocoon of happiness that surrounded her, and as she lay there, she relived the enjoyment of the day's outing and the unallayed pleasure she had derived from simply being in Nathan's company.

In time, however, Morpheus triumphed, and Eugenia's eyelids grew heavy, forcing her to pack away the wonderful memory—store it in that part of her heart that would protect it for years to come. She was almost asleep when a knock sounded at her door. Thinking it was Fiona, Eugenia called permission to enter.

"Forgive the intrusion," Nathan said, stepping into the room, "but I have had a letter from London, and I must return there immediately. It had been my hope to show you more of Hertfordshire, but I—"

Nathan stopped mid-sentence, for Eugenia had risen from the day bed, and only then did he realize that she wore nothing but a thin lawn wrapper. She had obviously finished her bath only minutes earlier, for the wisps of hair that framed her face were still wet from the steam, and the idea of her standing before him, still warm from the water, made it difficult for him to remember what he had been about to say.

Nor could he take his eyes from the wrapper that clung to her beautifully rounded hips and thighs. Unable to ignore the perfection of her form, he stared at her like some callow youth, one who had never been privy to the sight of a female in dishabille.

It might have been easier to regain his composure if her hair had not been loose. Unfortunately, the thick tousled locks tumbled down over her shoulders much as they might have done if she had lain asleep in his arms, and he—

Whoa! he told himself. *Get a rein on those thoughts before they run away with you.*

Fortunately, the object of his rampant imagination was unaware of his stampeding lust, and she stopped only inches from him, concern in her eyes. "What has happened?" she asked.

Nathan was obliged to concentrate upon her outstretched hand; otherwise he might have given in to the temptation to take her in his arms. All his primitive instincts urged him to gather her close so he could feel her soft body pressed against him, to bury his face in those thick strands of still damp hair, to tilt her face up so he might—

"You mentioned a letter," she said, bringing Nathan's wayward thoughts back to the letter from his butler, the reason he had come to speak with Eugenia.

"Yes. It is from London. Riddle sent it by special messenger, and it arrived this afternoon while we were at the ruins. It seems there was a break-in at the town house last evening."

Eugenia's hand went to her throat. "How awful. Was anyone hurt?"

Nathan shook his head. "Riddle thought he heard something and went to investigate. When the thief saw him, he ran."

"Thief? Was something taken? I pray it was not anything of special importance to you."

"As far as the servants can tell, the thief entered only one room. Yours. He stole your jewelry."

Her face seemed to drain of all color. "Not Henrietta's garnets? She was so kind to lend them to me. How am I ever to replace them?"

"What? No. The garnets are still there. Apparently the fellow was after something a bit more pricey, for he took the pieces you wore to the masked ball. The bracelet, the necklace, and the earrings. Riddle found the black leather jeweler's case on the floor outside your bedchamber door, but the contents were missing."

"Oh, Nathan. I am so sorry. Now you will not be able to return them to the jeweler."

This surprised him. "Why the deuce should I want to return them?"

"Because you . . . What I mean is . . ." She faltered over the words. "I should not have left them on the dressing table."

"I bought the set for you, Eugenia. Where you choose to leave it is your own affair. Or rather, it was."

She stared at him as if unable to comprehend what he had said. "You bought them for *me*? The diamond pendant? The teardrop earrings? I . . . I thought they were a loan. I did not understand. No one ever gave me . . ."

She took a deep breath, as if needing the air down in the depths of her lungs. "Thank you, Nathan," she said quietly. Then, as if years of training came to her rescue, she pulled her hand from his and stepped back, her spine ramrod straight. "Of course, I could not possibly accept anything so valuable."

"The point is moot, madam, since the items are gone, possibly forever. Be that as it may, I realized later that the gift was totally inappropriate. When I purchased them, I was not thinking, and for that apparent lack of perspicacity, I feel I should apologize."

"No, no. Really. You owe me no apology."

While she spoke, Nathan reached inside his coat and removed a small red velvet pouch. The pile of the cloth was rubbed thin with age, and the string that held it closed was frayed and showed knots in two places where it had been broken. "I should like you to have this," he said, "as a memento of your visit to Swanleigh Hall."

Eugenia opened her mouth to say something, but Nathan put his finger across her lips to stay the words.

"Before you refuse out of hand, allow me to tell you that the item has very little actual value. It is the kind of thing anyone might give you."

Having said this, he loosened the string on the pouch, caught her hand and turned it over, then dumped the contents of the pouch onto her palm. Only one item fell out, a thin brooch. It was less than two inches high, and it was made of silver wrought in the form of a swan.

Eugenia stared first at the brooch, then at Nathan. "Oh," she said, the single word little more than a whisper. "It is beautiful."

"It was my grandmother's," he said. "My father's mother. You and she have much in common."

"We do?"

He nodded. "Grandmother was outspoken, opinionated, and argumentative." At Eugenia's raised eyebrow, he hurried to add, "And like you, she was enchanted by Verulamium. She loved the swans, too, of course; that is why my grandfather gave her this little memento. She wore it all the time. I think Grandmother would have liked knowing her pin was worn by a young lady who shared her tastes."

"Did you like her?" Eugenia asked.

He shook his head. "I adored her. She was the only person I ever loved."

Eugenia waited to see if he would add anything to that very personal remark. When he did not, she turned the little pin over in her hand, admiring the swan's slender, graceful neck and its delicately etched feathers. "Are you quite certain you wish me to have this?"

"Quite certain."

He took the little silver bird from Eugenia's hand and opened the clasp. When he looked at her, as if asking permission, she smiled, and without another word he lifted the collar of her wrapper and fastened the swan in the folds of the white lawn.

"There," he said. "Now you have a reminder of your visit."

"Thank you," she said. "I shall treasure it always, though I need no reminder of my visit." She touched the little pin, and for a moment she felt tears sting her eyes. She forced herself not to blink and send the tears spilling down her cheeks. "I assure you," she said, "I shall never forget Swanleigh Hall."

Nathan left for London within the half hour, and the next day Eugenia spent the morning writing out the two dozen invitations for the very select card party to be held in ten days. Each time she penned Nathan's name upon the white pasteboard, she missed him a little more, and each time she inserted an invitation into its cover sheet and affixed the wafer, she grew a little sadder that her time with Nathan had been cut short by his return to town.

Nathan had asked Mr. Winfield to remain at the Hall to keep Eugenia company, but after Winny supplied her with the directions of the gentlemen who were to be honored with an invitation to the party, he asked if she would object to his riding over to Trillin Manor to pay his respects to Sir James and Lady Trillin.

"Not at all," she had replied.

"You are quite certain you do not mind?"

"Quite certain." Unable to stop herself, she touched the little silver pin that was all but hidden in the folds of her fichu. "After I finish here, I believe I shall take a stroll down to the lake."

"Just the thing. Lovely day for a walk." He was halfway out the door when a happy thought struck him and he turned back. "I say, Miss Eugenia, do you suppose Miss Trillin would like to see the swans? Should I suggest it, do you think?"

"If I know aught of the matter," Eugenia replied, "Dora would like it excessively. Perhaps you might ask Lady Trillin if she would allow Dora to join me for tea tomorrow afternoon."

"Capital idea!"

While Winny hastened to Trillin Manor to visit the lady with the big blue eyes, Eugenia took a leisurely stroll to the lake, where she gave herself up to thoughts whose entire focus was Nathan Seymour. At that same time, some thirty miles away in London, Nathan entered the Bow Street establishment of Sir John Fielding and asked to speak to someone about hiring a runner.

Nathan was shown to a stark but serviceable room furnished with nothing more than a deal table—upon which lay a pad of paper and a pencil—and two ladder-back chairs. Twenty minutes later, he was joined there by a red-haired fellow with a gold toothpick held between his lips and a neck the size of a Hereford bull's. The man was perhaps forty, but extremely fit, and he had obviously been a pugilist at some earlier time in his life. His oft-broken nose gave him away, that and a rather vicious-looking scar that bisected his left eyebrow, making the thick growth of reddish hair look like two separate entities.

"Arnold's the name, sir. I understand you've 'ad some jewelry stolen from your 'ouse in Grosvenor Square."

"That is correct."

"Well, now, Mr. Seymour, before I can begin my investigation, I'll need a description of the missing pieces. And if you've no objections, I should like to know the approximate value of the stolen merchandise."

"About a thousand pounds," Nathan replied, "but the return of the jewelry is of only secondary importance. What I wish you to discover for me is the whereabouts of the thief. I want to know where he lives and what places he frequents. And I am especially interested in the identity of any of his associates."

The runner gave Nathan a questioning look that raised the bisected eyebrow, but when no further information was forthcoming, he removed the gold toothpick from between his lips and slipped the item into the right breast pocket of his red vest. "I will do my best, sir. Have you any information on this felon?"

"It so happens I do. As the thief fled from the town house, my butler managed to get a good look at him. The servant recognized the man, for they had met once before. The fellow's name is Jem Weems, and he claims to be the uncle of one of the chambermaids."

Chapter Thirteen

Nathan remained in town for a full week. It was not his original plan, and to any who asked why he had delayed his return to Hertfordshire, he gave as his excuse his desire to attend a dinner party at White's, a dinner at which the honored guest was the Prussian hero, Field Marshal Blücher. His real reason, of course, was so that he might confer with the Bow Street Runner.

"I found Weems all right and tight," the runner said. "Wasn't too difficult. A weasel like that, 'e makes enemies. Enemies what'll spill all they know for tuppence."

He removed a small notebook from inside his coat. "Weems wasn't 'ard to locate. 'E cohabits with a female of ill repute in 'er place down by the docks. 'E's known to associate with any number of low types, most especially a sweep who goes by the name of Bertie O'Dell. And if Weems 'as got employment—I won't call it honest work—it'll be at a brothel on Pev'ny Lane. Most days, 'e goes there for several hours."

Arnold paused for a moment, and the bisected eyebrow twitched. When he spoke again, it was with obvious distaste. "That brothel, it's one of them as don't employ grown women. None but children there, and not a one of them older than ten or eleven years."

Nathan was not surprised to discover this link between

Weems and the brothel from which Fiona had escaped. "The owner of the place—did you discover his name?"

"No, sir. I was unable to ascertain the mort's 'andle, but I saw 'im right and tight, through a window at the rear of the brothel. No mistakin' that 'e was the owner, for 'e was 'anding over a bit of the ready—your pardon, sir, money I should say—to Weems."

The runner put his notebook back in his pocket. "I glimmed the mort's face, though, and I'll know 'is name before next we meet, or mine isn't Zebulon Arnold. Fancy dressed 'e was, like a gentleman. Though there's gentlemen and there's gentlemen, if you get my meanin'."

"I understand you perfectly," Nathan said. "I wonder, could you describe the man?"

"Yes, sir. 'E's a tall mort, some three or four years older than yourself, and 'e's quite slim, though I'll wager 'e strips to advantage. Some might call 'im 'andsome, but I'd not be among their number. 'Is 'air is black and wavy, and 'is eyes are even darker than 'is 'air. Black as coal them orbs be, and as 'ard and unfeelin' as Satan's own."

Nathan returned to Hertfordshire with only time enough to spend one night at Swanleigh Hall before escorting Eugenia back to town. During his week in London, he had thought of her often. For some reason, the town house had seemed empty without her. He had lived there alone for at least a dozen years, yet now, each time he went out and returned, he half expected to see Eugenia descending the narrow staircase, coming to greet him. Idiocy, of course. Almost as idiotic as that little stab of disappointment he felt when she was never there.

Everywhere he looked something reminded him of her. When he sat at the mahogany dining table, he pictured her sitting across from him, the small silver teapot beside her plate. In his imagination she was smiling at him over her teacup, or amusing him with something she had over-heard on the street or read in the *Times*.

After dinner, when he returned to the drawing room, she was there as well, a candelabrum beside her chair and a book in her hand. Of course, when she saw him, she always put the book aside; in fact, she discarded it happily, for she was eager as he to continue some earlier conversation.

Worst of all, he was haunted by the picture of her as he had seen her last, still damp from her bath and clad only in the plain, white lawn wrapper, her hair swinging free and inviting a man to run his fingers through it. Each night, when he lay in the ornately carved tester bed that had been his grandfather's, Nathan pictured Eugenia coming to him, her hair loose and the wrapper both concealing and revealing her delectable curves. She always hesitated just inside the room, a shy smile upon her lips and some unnamed emotion in her brown eyes.

He was unfamiliar with the emotion. It was one he had never seen before, yet each time he saw it, it left him feeling as though he had been dealt a telling blow to the solar plexus. Each time, when Eugenia came to him, he tried to understand why she looked at him in that way, and when he was unsuccessful, the picture of her would slowly disappear.

Afterward, when the vision had vanished into the ether from which it had come, Nathan lay in his ornately carved bed and steeled himself against the ache that always followed. It was an ache he did not understand, for it went all the way to his soul, yet he knew, somehow, that it had everything to do with that look in Eugenia's eyes.

Upon his return to Swanleigh Hall, he finally found Eugenia waiting for him. He had been greeted at the door by Avery, but when Nathan asked where his guests might be found, the butler informed him that Mr. Winfield had ridden off quite early in the day.

"His destination, I believe, was Trillin Manor."

"And Miss Bailey?"

"Miss Bailey is in the library, sir."

By that time Nathan had entered the vestibule, and something made him glance down the corridor where it turned the corner to the east wing. Eugenia stood there, looking her usual calm self, waiting for him much as he had pictured her waiting on the stairs at the town house. He touched his finger to his forehead in salute and was rewarded with a warm, friendly smile.

After handing his hat and gloves to the butler, he went directly to Eugenia. "Hello," he said.

"Hello, Nathan," she replied. "Welcome home."

"Ecod, Nate!" Mr. Winfield said upon hearing that the thief was none other than Jem Weems. "What cheek. Have they caught the fellow?"

"As to that, Winny, I cannot say. I am having him followed, so the moment he attempts to sell the jewelry, he will be apprehended. Until that time, I am content to keep him under surveillance, where he can do no mischief."

Eugenia sat her fork on her plate, for her appetite, as well as her festive mood, was destroyed by the information that it was Weems who had been in her bedchamber. "Surely there must be dozens of far more valuable items he might have stolen. Why, I wonder, was he satisfied with nothing more than the diamond set?"

Nathan pushed aside the salmon with red wine and nutmeg sauce, and signaled the footman to take his plate away. "I believe Weems's motive was more revenge than thievery. You outwitted him, Eugenia, possibly causing him to lose face among his low-life fellows. It is altogether possible that he wanted to get his own back, as it were, by searching your room and taking something so you would know he had been there. He wished to frighten you."

Eugenia shivered. "He succeeded. I cannot like the thought that he was there, or that he touched my things. But my feelings aside, what of Fiona? Need we be concerned for her?"

"I think not. She is safe here in Hertfordshire. And I hope you will not be concerned for your own safety. I am confident that Weems will make an error soon enough—an error that will result in his arrest and ultimate deportation."

"I hope you may be right."

Nathan lifted his wineglass. "Enough talk of things unpleasant. Come, let us make a toast to friends reunited."

Winny and Eugenia followed his example and lifted their glasses. "To friends reunited," they repeated.

When the toast was drunk, Nathan asked them if they could be ready to leave for London before noon the next day.

"Of course," Eugenia replied. "I need only dash off a note of farewell to Dora Trillin, then I will be quite ready."

"Be more than happy to deliver the note for you," Winny said, his voice studiously nonchalant. "I am persuaded I left my, er, my gloves there this afternoon. Meant to go round tomorrow to fetch them, but perhaps I would do better to go this evening."

Nathan exchanged glances with Eugenia before replying to his old friend's none-too-subtle excuse for visiting Dora Trillin. "An excellent notion, Winny. Please give Sir James and Lady Trillin my regards. And Miss Trillin as well."

Since Winny had already tossed his napkin on the table and was preparing to quit the dining room that very moment, Nathan was obliged to smother a smile. "Do not, I pray you, have the least concern for Eugenia and me. If we set our minds to it, I am certain she and I can find some way to entertain ourselves until your return."

Apparently, sarcasm was lost on a gentleman in the throes of love, and Winny took the remark at face value. "Whatever you do," he said good-naturedly, "do not play cards with her."

"Oh?" Nathan said, hiding another smile, "is this the voice of experience? Am I to understand that you have tried your skill against hers?"

"Haven't I just. At the last tally, I owned Miss Eugenia in excess of seven million pounds."

As it transpired, Nathan was called away soon after Winny left. One of his tenants had caught a thief in his poultry house and had come to Nathan to ask what he should do with the fellow. As a consequence, Eugenia was left alone, and at nine o'clock, after the tea tray was brought in and the gentlemen still had not returned, she gave up hope of any private time with Nathan.

It wanted but two days until the card party—fifty hours to be exact—and while the number of hours she and Nathan might spend together dwindled, something seemed to be growing inside Eugenia's chest, squeezing painfully upon her heart. Sitting there waiting for Nathan to come home only added to the pain, so reluctantly she took herself up to her bedchamber.

As a consequence, she did not see Nathan again until the three of them climbed into the carriage the next day for the return journey to London. She had so wanted to be alone with him for those three hours, but reason told her that Mr. Winfield could not be expected to travel alone when there was ample room for him in the chaise.

Yesterday, when Nathan arrived at Swanleigh Hall, Eugenia had been frighteningly happy to see him. She had been reading in the library when she heard the coachman taking the carriage around to the stables. With a speed that was embarrassing, she had tossed aside her book and sped down the corridor, stopping only when she heard Nathan asking where she might be found.

Then he had seen her. He touched his forehead in salute, and Eugenia breathed a sign of contentment. Nathan was back, and all was right with her world again. But she had not had a moment's privacy with him, and now here they were, the three of them, traveling back to the town house.

Time was running out for her. At nine o'clock tomorrow night, the card party would be held. That was thirty hours hence, and after the party, Eugenia would return to the school.

As the crow flew, the distance between Grosvenor Square and the Misses Becknell's Academy was not great. Unfortunately, the crow was not the only measurer of distance. Once Eugenia was back in the little village south of the Thames, back at her job as instructress in fine needle work, deportment, and the uses of the globe, an uncrossable chasm would separate her from Mr. Nathan Seymour. She was not fool enough to believe she would ever traverse that gulf again, and unable to span the abyss, she would never again see the man she loved.

These thoughts plagued her during the journey, and by late afternoon, when they arrived in Grosvenor Square, she was cast into an unrelieved fit of the dismals.

"I will just stop by my rooms, Nate," Winny said, "and wait for you there."

"No, I will come with you. Allow me to escort Eugenia inside first. I will be but a moment."

Eugenia was being handed down from the carriage while this exchange took place, so by the simple expedient of lowering her gaze, she was able to hide her disappointment from the gentlemen. Self-deception was not so easy. Whatever was inside her chest, squeezing painfully at her heart, increased twofold, leaving her very close to tears.

Was she never to have another hour alone with Nathan?

Riddle met her at the door, welcoming her back. "I trust you enjoyed your stay at Swanleigh Hall."

"I should be hard to please if I had not. I could be wrong, but I believe Hertfordshire must be the most beautiful of all the counties."

"I could not agree with you more," Nathan said, coming past the wide oak door just behind her, "and I mean to return there just as soon as this card party has come and gone."

"Speaking of the party, sir," the butler said, "a number of response cards have arrived. I left them on the side table in the drawing room. Shall I bring some refreshments in there?"

"None for me, thank you. Mr. Winfield is waiting for me. However, Miss Eugenia is probably in sore need of a cup of tea." He turned to Eugenia then, with a smile so warm it positively melted away that constriction around her heart. "Would you mind going through the acceptances and making a list of those guests who are coming?"

"No," she replied, "I do not mind at all."

From the speed with which she agreed to his request, Eugenia decided it was as well he had not asked her to commit some heinous crime. It really was not fair for a man to have such a devastating smile!

"I shall bring the tea directly, Miss Eugenia," Riddle promised.

When the servant reached the rear of the vestibule and disappeared through the doorway leading to the kitchen area, Nathan lifted Eugenia's hand to his lips. "Forgive me, my friend, for leaving all this tedious business for you to handle. I would stay here to offer you my assistance, but Winny and I are off to Bow Street to speak with someone about an extra runner. I thought it might make you feel less nervous about the invasion of your privacy if someone was watching the house."

"It would," she said. "You are very kind."

"And will you be equally kind, madam, and agree to join me for dinner this evening? There will be just the two of us."

He could not have said anything more guaranteed to lift her spirits, and she hurried to assure him that she would be delighted to dine with him.

"I shall look forward to it," he said.

Eugenia watched him drive away, then went abovestairs to change her traveling dress before looking at the invitation responses. Though Nathan was gone most of the afternoon, Eugenia went about her tasks happily, for she knew that when he returned, they would have the evening together.

She dressed with care, donning her modest, pale gold sarcenet and Henrietta Parker's garnets; then she pinned the little silver swan in her hair, just above her right ear. Feeling lighthearted and joyous, she completed her toilette, then descended the stairs and went directly to the drawing room.

Nathan stood before the fireplace, studying the marble statue of Urania, which occupied the niche to his right, and when he turned to greet Eugenia, the light in his eyes told her he was recalling their conversation more than a week ago in the hall at Swanleigh. At that time he had told her she resembled the statue of the Muse.

"Good evening," he said, making her a gallant bow. "Dressed as you are tonight, you put me in mind of the gold-leafed Muse."

After curtsying, she said, "Pray, how am I to respond to that observation, sir? Especially when I recall that you told me you much preferred the marble statue."

"When speaking of statues, I do prefer the marble to the gold, but neither of those materials can compare to a real flesh-and-blood Urania—especially one who possesses the requisite brown eyes."

Though Eugenia found nothing to dislike in this very pleasing line of conversation, it caused the warmth to permeate her cheeks; thus, she was not too unhappy when Riddle chose that moment to announce that dinner was served.

During the meal, they spoke mostly of Hertfordshire and what Eugenia had done to occupy her time while Nathan was in town. For her part, she cared little what they discussed. It was enough for her just to be alone with Nathan.

In time, of course, they spoke of the coming card party. Every one of the two dozen guests had accepted the invitation, and it occurred to Eugenia that for all his reputation as a scoundrel, Nathan must be well liked. At least by twenty-three of the men invited. She already knew Lord Durham's feelings where Nathan was concerned, and they were not admiring.

"Lord Durham is coming," she said, watching Nathan's face to see how he received the news. There was a nearly imperceptible hesitation in his breathing; otherwise, his countenance remained unruffled, his manner urbane.

"That was the plan, was it not? To bring Durham here so you might defeat him at cards and win back your cousin's ten thousand?"

"Yes, that was the plan. However, if I had known how much you disliked his lordship, and how deserving he was of your abhorrence, I would not have asked for your assistance in the matter."

A smile tugged at the corners of Nathan's mouth. "If memory serves me, madam, you came to me because you needed a scoundrel to teach you how to catch a scoundrel."

Eugenia felt heat rush to her face. "Please, do not remind me of my words. As you told me at that time, you and Lord Durham are nothing alike."

He chuckled. "Are you telling me you no longer think me a scoundrel?"

She dare not tell Nathan what she truly thought of him, that she loved him with all her heart, so she evaded his question. Instead, she said, "I will speak only of Lord Durham, for I now feel 'scoundrel' is too temperate a term for the man. Had he done only half the things you told me of him, he would still be deserving of the name villain."

She was silent for several minutes, nervous suddenly about the following night. When Nathan offered her sixpence for her thoughts, she asked if she might postpone the sale until the meal was finished and they were in the drawing room.

Though he raised his eyebrow in question, he said nothing, merely placed his napkin beside his plate to indicate that he was quite finished. "We can go now if you like."

"Yes. Please."

"Riddle?"

"Yes, sir."

"Bring Miss Eugenia's tea to the drawing room. I will have my port in there as well. After that, please see that we are not disturbed."

"As you wish, sir."

Nathan gave her his arm and led her from the dining room. While she disposed herself upon the pale green settee, he crossed to the empty fireplace and leaned his back against the mantel. As if by mutual consent, they refrained from speaking, choosing instead to wait until Riddle had set the small teapot and a cup and saucer on the piecrust table beside her, then served Nathan his glass of port. Only after the butler had bowed himself out, did Eugenia confess to her misgivings.

"What if this entire scheme goes awry?"

"And why should it do that?"

"Because I have serious doubts about my ability to charm Lord Durham into playing cards with me."

"You charmed me. Why should Durham be any less susceptible?"

Eugenia shook her head. "I did not charm you into testing your skill against mine, and well you know it. I told you I could not be bested, then I *challenged* you to try your luck. Unfortunately, such tactics will not work with Lord Durham, for he must not suspect that I could defeat him. No man would risk being defeated by a woman while twenty-three other gentlemen are watching."

"I see your point. So what do you propose?"

"You told me yourself," she continued, "that his lordship plays cards with females for only one reason, because he wishes to seduce them once the game is ended. Therefore, if I am to be allowed to sit at Durham's table, I will first be obliged to make him wish to make love to me. And I . . . I will need you to show me how to do so."

"Damnation, Eugenia!"

Nathan could not believe how angry Eugenia's request made him. He felt his empty hand ball into a fist, and he longed to put that fist through Cedric Durham's face.

"You do not need to attract the likes of Durham."

"Yes," she said quietly, "I do."

He glared at her, hoping his anger would dissuade her. It did not.

"You promised, Nathan, to give me lessons, and so far you have given me only two. You showed me how to attract a man's attention, and you taught me to dance the waltz. Now, teach me how to make Durham wish to seduce me. Let this be the final lesson."

"No."

"Please," she said, her eyes imploring him, "teach me what I must do, else this will all have been for naught."

Though Nathan wished he had never agreed to this cursed scheme, he was unable to resist the pleading in those warm brown eyes. "Deuce take it, Eugenia."

"Show me," she said softly, "how to make a man wish to take me to his bed."

Chapter Fourteen

Show me how to make a man wish to take me to his bed.

The very words caused a pulse in Nathan's temple to throb painfully; at the same time, the request, so innocently made, lit a fire in his belly. Teach her! Heaven help him—every night for the last two weeks he had dreamed of nothing else but taking her to bed.

His bed!

Though he was tempted to throw the glass of wine across the room, smashing the crystal into a thousand pieces, he managed to control his anger sufficiently to set the goblet upon the mantel. When she continued to look at him with those wide, naive eyes, Nathan knew he must complete the lessons. What else could he do? He had, after all, given her his word.

"There is," he said, his manner not at all conciliatory, "a certain unspoken communication, a knowing look that passes between a man and a woman."

"A look," she repeated, her attention fixed upon his words.

"Yes. At first their eyes may meet quite by accident—across a table or across a room—the circumstances do not matter. Once the contact is made, however, if the woman does not look away, then the man will take a second, longer look."

"Always?" Eugenia asked.

"Always," he replied. "It is the nature of the beast."

When he paused, she said, "Please, go on."

"Of course," he continued, "anyone might return a gaze for a few seconds and mean little by it, but when those few seconds have passed, and the woman continues to look at the man, he begins to think she might be interested in him." He took a moment to adjust his cravat; somehow, it had become rather snug. "Interested on, er, a purely physical level."

"Then," Eugenia prompted.

"Then, to test the idea that the woman may be interested in him, the man will give her a questioning look, as if to say, 'Shall I pursue?' If she answers with a half smile, he knows there is a strong chance he can coax her into allowing him to escort her home."

"And if the woman does not answer his questioning look with a smile?"

"If she does not smile, yet continues to maintain eye contact with him, the man begins to search about in his mind for the answer to two questions. Where is the nearest empty room? And how quickly can he get the woman into that room?"

Eugenia's face went bright pink, but she did not flinch at Nathan's outspokenness. Instead, she said, "I see that I must, under no circumstance, forget to smile."

Her attempt at humor failed, and to control his anger at the thought of her smiling at Cedric Durham, Nathan was obliged to reclaim his wineglass. He downed the port in one continuous swallow, and when he set the empty goblet upon the mantel and turned back to face Eugenia, she had risen from the settee and was standing quite still, looking at him.

Their eyes met, and she did not look away.

Taken by surprise, Nathan sought to read her purpose. While he stared at her, a hint of pink colored her cheeks, and though she lowered her gaze, she lifted it again almost immediately. This time, when blue-gray met brown, Nathan felt as if he had been dealt a blow to the chest, for the blend of innocence and expectation in Eugenia's eyes quite knocked the breath from his lungs.

Damn her! Why does she not look away? I did not give her leave to practice on me.

An eternity passed, and Nathan began to suspect that the lesson had ended and something else was taking place. He warned himself not to put a name to that something else, yet the possibility was driving him mad—the possibility that Eugenia wanted him as much as he wanted her.

She continued to hold his gaze, and Nathan, unable to look away himself, found his control stretched further and further. Then she touched the tip of her tongue to her bottom lip, as if to moisten it, and like an elastic pulled to its limit, his control finally broke.

"Eugenia," he said, his voice raw with desire. "Do you know what you are doing?"

When she nodded, he covered the distance between them in two long strides and caught her by the shoulders, pulling her against his chest. "Beautiful Eugenia," he said, then bent his head and captured her lips. He kissed her, and she kissed him back, shyly, but eagerly, and the sweetness of it nearly drove him mad.

While their kisses mingled, Eugenia slipped her arms around Nathan's waist, wanting to hold him close, as he was holding her. He broke the kiss finally, and with his mouth pressed against her temple, he whispered, "My sweet, wonderful girl."

His words were like the music of heaven to her ears, and Eugenia sighed with pleasure. Nathan loved her as she loved him; knowing this, she felt certain that nothing in this world could match her happiness. She wanted to stay in his arms forever.

To her disappointment, he put his hands on her shoulders and slowly pushed her away so he could look down into her face. "Forget the card party," he said. "I will cancel it—then you and I can go back to Swanleigh Hall. I never got to show you all that is beautiful in Hertford-shire."

It was exactly what Eugenia wanted to do, but if they canceled the party, how was she to win back the ten thousand pounds? "We cannot cancel it."

"Of course we can," he said. "Nothing easier."

She shook her head. "I want that ten thousand."

From the questioning look on Nathan's face, she knew he was puzzled by her adamancy, but how could she explain to him her need to return the money to her aunt. He was a wealthy man, and he would never understand a young girl's humiliation at having been a poor relation, unwanted and barely tolerated. She needed to expunge that memory. It was a matter of pride—she needed to do it for herself as well as for the honor of her parents.

"If the money means that much to you," he said, gathering her in his arms again and settling her head upon his chest, "I will give it to you. Forget the party, and we can—"

"*You* will give it to me?" She lifted her head so she could look up into his face. "Just like that, you would hand over ten thousand pounds? A small fortune?"

"Do not be concerned. I can afford it. If the truth be known," he said, his tone deprecating, as though he told a joke on himself, "in my callow youth, I once spent that much on an emerald bracelet."

He had bought an emerald bracelet? For whom?

Even before the question was completely formed in Eugenia's mind, she knew the answer: He had bought the bracelet for one of his mistresses.

A mistress.

He had bought one an emerald necklace, and now he was willing to give another the money outright. It was

Nathan's way of telling Eugenia he wanted her for his new mistress.

Like a pebble bouncing down a mountainside, that word reverberated inside her brain. *Mistress, mistress, mistress* it said as it bounced from one rocky outcrop to another, picking up momentum until it landed with a painful thud inside Eugenia's heart. Two minutes ago she had thought nothing could match her happiness. She had been wrong. The pain in her heart not only matched that previous joy; it obliterated it.

When Nathan had kissed her and whispered sweet words to her, she had thought he loved her as she loved him. She thought he wanted to marry her, to spend the rest of his life with her. What a fool she had been. He did not want a wife; he wanted another mistress.

Tears burned at the back of her eyes, But Eugenia willed them not to fall. She would not cry. Not here. Not now. Nathan still held her in his arms, but when she put her hands on his chest and pushed, he let her go.

Surprise was writ plainly on his face. "What is it, my sweet? Is something—"

"Your offer," she said, "I am afraid I cannot accept it. I must win the money from Lord Durham, or it loses its value to me and to my purpose. And now," she continued, stepping back, putting some distance between them, "I pray you will excuse me, for I find I have an excruciating headache."

Without another word, Eugenia turned and strode rather quickly from the drawing room. Not bothering to take one of the candles from the console table, she sped up the dimly lit stairs and hurried to her bedchamber, where she turned the key in the lock to ensure her privacy.

Not taking the time to remove her dinner dress, she threw herself facedown upon the bed and gave vent to the tears she had been holding back since she realized that

Nathan wanted her for his mistress. She cried as she had not done since the death of her parents.

In time, of course, the tears finally ceased to flow. They always did. No matter how overwhelming the trials life visits upon a person, the tears finally dry up. Experience told Eugenia this was true. When all was said and done, what was the point in crying? All the tears in the world would not change the fact that Nathan's feelings for her were not love.

When she could think more rationally, Eugenia knew she had only herself to blame for the misunderstanding. She had failed to remember what she had overheard the first night she spent in this house. She had stood at the bottom of the stairs and eavesdropped while Nathan remonstrated with Winny for having invited Eugenia to the theater. He had warned his friend that he might have encouraged her to believe the invitation might lead to something more serious.

"She is a schoolmistress," Nathan had said, "and by her own admission she is not privy to the ways of society. Once the card party is a thing of the past, I am persuaded it would be wisest to let the lady return to that sphere to which she belongs."

With those remembered words in her ears, Eugenia lit a candle and went to the washstand to splash cold water on her puffy eyes. Nathan had been in the right of it; she belonged in a completely different sphere—a sphere where love was given freely, but could, under no circumstances, be purchased.

"And the minute the party is over," she warned the tear-stained face in the small looking glass, "you will return to that sphere."

Chapter Fifteen

The following day, Eugenia remained in her room until
time to go down for the party. She refused all but a tea
tray brought to her by Riddle that afternoon, while all
other entreaties at her door went unanswered, even those
from Nathan Seymour himself.

At five minutes to nine, she took one last look at herself in the looking glass, applied just a bit more powder
to her face, freshened the lip rouge, then added a second
heart-shaped patch. The first was to the right of her
mouth; the second was in the hollow of her left shoulder,
where the square neck of the evening dress left her skin
exposed.

Attired once again in one of Henrietta Parker's dresses,
a primrose georgette with small puff sleeves and a bodice
so tight it very nearly pushed her bosom over the top of
the low neckline, Eugenia looked every inch the lightskirt. She fastened the garnets around her neck, but this
time she was not so naive as to believe they would divert
anyone's attention from her décolletage.

At the last moment, she pinned the little silver swan in
her hair. It was a reminder of a happy time, and it gave
her courage.

Not wanting to be alone with Nathan, she had waited
until she knew the guests had begun to arrive. Now, as
Eugenia descended the stairs, she heard laughter and the

sound of masculine voices coming from the drawing room. Riddle stood at the entrance, ensuring that only those with invitations were admitted, and the doors to the three ground-floor rooms stood open. At least a hundred candles were lit, and the vestibule and the three rooms were as bright as day.

After taking a deep, fortifying breath, Eugenia crossed the vestibule and entered the drawing room. She stopped just inside the doorway, taken aback by the change in the decor, for the usual furnishings had been removed. In their place were five square gaming tables and two round ones, each covered with green baize. The square tables, meant for whist, had chairs for four, while the round tables, meant for loo or vingt-un, had places for six, with extra chairs along the walls.

At least twenty guests milled about the room, but Eugenia had eyes for only one man. She spied Nathan standing beside the niche containing the Muse Urania; he was listening intently to something a short, balding gentleman said. Eugenia had never seen Nathan look more handsome. He wore a maroon coat, a silver-striped waistcoat, and silver gray knee breeches. The light from a nearby candelabrum shone upon his light brown hair, and as she watched him, he seemed to sense her presence, for he looked up, those gray eyes staring straight at her.

He excused himself to the balding gentleman and came directly to Eugenia, capturing her hand, then leaning close, his words for her ears alone. "I ask you once again to forget about gambling with Durham. Turn around this instant and return to your room."

Eugenia shook her head. "I cannot."

The lips that had kissed hers with such tenderness and such heart-stopping passion the night before now appeared grim, almost angry. "Very well," he said, "since you will not leave, will you make me a promise?"

"If I can."

"After you have won your ten thousand, will you leave the table immediately?"

"I will do that. I want only what Lord Durham won from my cousin, not a groat more."

"And will you promise one other thing?"

"Yes."

"When you quit the table, will you go directly to your bedchamber and lock the door? Lock it and not open it again until morning?"

"But, I—" She stopped, not wanting to tell him that she planned to leave as soon as the party was over.

"No matter who knocks," he said, "do not open the door to anyone."

"If that is your wish," she said. "I will do as you ask."

Nathan had to be content with that. He had no idea what he had said or done last evening to make her freeze him out like a February ice storm, then refuse to speak to him today, but he would try to solve that riddle tomorrow. For tonight, it was imperative that he ensure her safety. With a man of Cedric Durham's ilk in the house, anything might happen, especially when a woman as beautiful as Eugenia had sworn to charm him.

Even painted up like a Cyprian, she was the most fascinating woman Nathan had ever seen, and it had needed all his restraint to remain calm, knowing that every man in the room would be ogling her lovely bosom.

Eugenia had refused to leave the party, but if Nathan saw her make eye contact with Lord Durham as she had made it with him last evening, he would not be responsible for the consequences. Nathan was not above tossing her over his shoulder and removing her from the room by force!

Actually, he liked that idea, and he was lost in thought, imagining himself carrying her up the stairs, when his attention was claimed by a trio of newly arrived guests. Reluctantly, he surrendered Eugenia's hand.

She escaped immediately, crossing the room to greet Henrietta Parker, who had brought along another female. The stranger, a slender woman in her early thirties, possessed unbelievably pale skin, improbably red hair, and a most impressive bosom. The card party was supposed to be an all-male occasion, but the two women were being paid to mingle with the guests so Eugenia's presence would not occasion remark.

"Hello," Eugenia said, happy to see Henrietta.

"My dear," the woman greeted her, taking Eugenia's hands in her gloved ones and drawing her close as if to kiss her on the cheek. "Did Nathan tell you the news?" she whispered.

When Eugenia shook her head, Henrietta whispered again. "He has found the person who set fire to my bedchamber. I do not know how it happened, but he has proof of the man's identity. The runners have the man under surveillance, and they hope to make an arrest within a matter of days. I shall have justice at last."

"Who was it?" Eugenia asked. Before she received an answer, however, one of the guests approached them.

"By Jove," the man said, bowing to Henrietta before eying Eugenia and the other woman, "a trio of beauties. Be a sport, Hen, and introduce me to your lovely friends."

"Oh, no, my lord," she replied, "I refuse to introduce you to anyone until you have procured for me a glass of Nathan's excellent champagne. You know how thirsty I get at these parties."

Ever resourceful, Henrietta avoided revealing Eugenia's name by catching the gentleman by one arm and her friend with the other and all but dragging the two of them to the dining room, where refreshments were set out.

Within minutes the guests began to settle down for some serious card playing, and soon all the tables were filled. Nathan stood near the pianoforte, engaged in con-

versation with Mr. Winfield, another gentleman, and the
woman with the dubious red hair, but if he felt Eugenia's
gaze, he gave no indication of it.

Searching the room, Eugenia finally spotted Lord
Durham at one of the round tables close to the front windows. He was dressed in unrelieved black, a circumstance that put her in mind of Beelzebub himself, and
even as she spied him, Durham looked up and saw her.
He inclined his head in greeting, then gave her an ac-
cessing look, scanning her from head to toe in a manner
that made her flesh crawl. Fortunately for Eugenia's
composure, his attention was recalled by the necessity of
placing a bet, and he gave his attention to the cards in his
hand.

She knew she must ultimately put herself within
"charming" distance of Lord Durham, so she decided to
circle the room. Moving in no particular pattern, she
stopped at each of the tables long enough to assess the
ability of the different players. One or two gentlemen
were skilled enough, but the rest were really rather
mediocre, for they either could not or would not keep
track of the discards. It baffled Eugenia why men with so
little aptitude for the game staked such large sums of
money on each hand. Surely, they must know they were
destined to lose it all.

At last she arrived at Lord Durham's table, where he
and five gentlemen were engrossed in a game of loo. Almost immediately the winning card was played, a ten of
trumps, and one of the players swore beneath his breath.
In all fairness, Eugenia could not fault the man for his
outburst, for he had not taken a single trick and was,
therefore, obliged to place five times the wager amount
into the pool.

Eugenia was astounded by the sum of money amassed
on a single hand. Even after the pool was divided by
those who had been lucky enough to take a trick—with

each player taking one fifth for each trick won—Lord Durham increased his winnings by a thousand pounds. So far, he appeared to be the most successful player at the table.

Since it was her goal to relieve his lordship of this night's winnings and more, Eugenia observed his style of play. He was good. At least she could absolve him from having cheated her cousin; there would have been no need to do so. Durham kept his mind on the game, never letting his emotions rule when wagering, and not by so much as a twitch did he give away his position. With the exception of Nathan, Cedric Durham was the best player in the room.

The best *male* player, she amended.

The gentleman who had sworn at his ill luck smiled up at Eugenia. "Come," he said, "allow me to draw up a chair for you. A handsome female at the table just might bring me luck."

"And you need all the luck you can get," remarked one of his cronies, cuffing him on the shoulder in a good-natured manner. "Another round like that, and I will have that bay gelding you've been refusing to sell me."

Pleased with the invitation, Eugenia seated herself. While the new dealer shuffled the deck, the gentleman serving as banker made a note on the tally sheet, then passed over another stack of chips to the man at her right. "That is another thousand to you, Richards."

A footman with a tray bearing a decanter of brandy and fresh glasses paused at the table. He must have been hired for the evening, for Eugenia had never seen him before. She could not help but stare, for he was a most unusual-looking fellow, with a neck the size of a large animal's and an eyebrow completely bisected by a scar.

Drinks were poured all around and the bottle set in the middle of the table. Play continued for another hour, and during that time, Eugenia noticed that while Lord

Durham often lifted his glass to his lips, he seldom actually drank anything. Others were not so careful, and before long the unlucky Mr. Richards was showing signs of inebriation.

"Come along, old chap," his friend said when the next hand was finished and Durham had taken the largest share of the pool, "I need some food. What say you, Richards, do you suppose Seymour has any of those lobster patties you are so fond of wolfing down?"

"Wait," said another man, shoving what was left of his chips toward the banker for tally. "Believe I will join you. Feel a need to stretch a bit."

The three of them rose from the table—Mr. Richards none too steadily—and disappeared in the direction of the dining room. With their departure, there remained at the table only Lord Durham, the banker, and the short, balding gentleman Nathan had been speaking with when Eugenia first entered the room. Both he and the banker had been mildly successful, but there was no question that Durham was the biggest winner.

The deal was changing hands, and as the banker shuffled the cards, Eugenia decided the time had come to try her luck. After saying a little prayer, she feigned a delicate sneeze. "Oh, dear," she said, looking directly at Lord Durham, "I seem to have misplaced my reticule. May I trouble you, my lord, for your handkerchief?"

"My pleasure, Papillion." Reaching into his pocket, he withdrew a clean square of linen and passed it to her.

As she took the proffered handkerchief, Eugenia let her fingers trail along the underside of Durham's hand, and when he looked up, a question in his eyes, she smiled.

"Thank you," she said. "I would have disliked being obliged to leave the table, for I do so love a game of loo." She pressed the linen to her nose, never losing eye contact with Durham. "I believe I told you, when we danced at the masked ball, that I am excessively fond of playing cards."

"Yes," he drawled, his glance sliding down to her low neckline, "I remember your mentioning that you numbered cards among your . . . uh, talents."

The insinuating tone of his voice, coupled with his overlong ogling of her bosom, made Eugenia feel decidedly queasy, and she thanked heaven that she was in a well-lit room filled with more than a dozen gentlemen. Even the thought of being alone with such a man as Durham made her shiver with revulsion. Trying to ignore her feelings of distaste, she said, "There are those who say I play rather well."

The hint was not lost on his lordship, and he placed his elbows on the table so he might lean toward her a little. When he spoke, his voice was low, suggestive of intimacy. "Since you have been so unfortunate as to misplace your reticule, pretty Papillion, I can only assume that if we included you in this hand, you would expect someone to frank you." He took another, more lingering look at her bosom. "If you should lose, my sweet, what have you to offer as collateral against your debt?"

"I know nothing of collateral," she said, lowering her lashes in a coy manner, "but never fear, my lord, I *always* pay my debts."

To her surprise, the balding gentleman suddenly took a stack of his own chips and set them on the table in front of her. "Here, ma'am," he said. "I will frank you for a hand or two."

"Oh, sir," she cooed, touching the chips. "Five hundred pounds—you are most truly the gentleman."

If the angry look in Durham's eyes was anything to go by, he was not at all pleased with the other man's intervention. When the banker said rather sharply, "Are we playing loo here, or are we having a tea party?" there seemed little Durham could do but give in.

"Deal the cards," he said.

The game began with the players putting their wagers into a pool, with twenty-five pounds being the required opening wager. Three cards were dealt each player, then two cards each, with the final card turned up to signify trumps. It was a four of diamonds.

"Ooh, ooh," Eugenia cooed. "Diamonds have always been lucky for me."

She looked at her first three cards. They were a five of diamonds, a six of diamonds, and an eight of hearts. The next two cards were a ten of diamonds and an ace of clubs. She decided to try for the "trump" flush. Only one flush could best it, that was a Pam-high flush.

The dealer asked the balding man his choice: Play this hand? Not play? Or take new cards? The man chose to play the hand he held.

When asked her choice, Eugenia placed the eight of hearts and the ace of clubs facedown on the table. "Two, please."

Lord Durham took one, and the dealer took three. Eugenia picked up her cards. The first was an ace of diamonds. She held her breath. Even if she did not get the flush, chances were she would take at least three of the tricks. Slowly, she lifted the final card. It was the Jack of clubs—Pam! The reigning wild card. Nothing could beat a Pam-high flush!

Schooling her face, she followed suit as everyone added another twenty-five pounds to the pool, which now totaled two hundred. "Before we begin playing for tricks," the dealer said, "does anyone wish to declare a flush?"

The balding man laid down a heart flush. "Queen high," he said, a look of satisfaction on his face. "Can anyone best it?"

"I believe so," Eugenia said, laying down her Pam-high diamond flush.

For an instant, all three men were silent; then the banker laughed aloud, drawing the attention of several people nearby, while the balding man congratulated her. "Well done, ma'am."

Lord Durham pushed the pool of two hundred pounds toward her. "So, Papillion," he said, "it appears that diamonds are, indeed, lucky for you."

Eugenia heard the condescension in his voice and knew he credited her win to beginner's luck. Let him think what he would; it mattered little to her, for she knew her ability. Furthermore, she was in the game now, and no matter at what point Lord Durham finally recognized her skill, he could hardly refuse to let her continue to play. Nor could he leave the table while she was winning, for to do so would be tantamount to branding himself unsportsmanlike.

Within the hour, Eugenia had amassed eight thousand pounds, five thousand of it from Lord Durham. The banker and the balding man admitted defeat and declared themselves spectators from that moment on, but they bore their losses gracefully. The remaining battle was left to Eugenia and Lord Durham, but if his lordship knew aught of losing gracefully, he kept the fact to himself. His face was a studied mask, but the look in his coal black eyes spoke of cold rage.

Remembering that the man was a bully of long standing, Eugenia felt a frisson of fear in the face of that rage. Thankfully, in the next moment she recalled that Durham had no idea of her identity or her real direction, and she breathed a sigh of relief. Let him rage; let him plan the wreaking of his vengeance. After tomorrow, he would never find her.

It was Eugenia's turn to deal, and amid the small crowd of spectators who had gathered around the table, she felt Nathan watching her. She never saw him. She never heard his voice. But she felt his presence. If the crowd had numbered twenty-four thousand, she would have known Nathan was there.

After shuffling the cards without fanfare, she let Durham cut. She decided to leave the deck in that spot where his lordship had set it; then, using only her right hand, she dealt the cards, slowly, carefully, so that all who watched could attest that none came from the bottom of the stack. Three and three she dealt, then two and two. The card she turned up for trumps was the ten of clubs.

While her cards still lay facedown upon the baize-covered table, she said, "Dealer's choice, Lord Durham. What say you to this being the last hand? Each player wagers two thousand pounds, with no raises to the pool."

He had already gathered his cards and looked at them, and now the tiniest of smiles betrayed his belief that she had just committed a tactical error. "As you say, ma'am, 'dealer's choice.'"

They each placed their wagers in the middle of the table; then Eugenia gathered her five cards and looked at them. In a clear voice, she asked, "Do you play, sir? Not play? Or do you wish to exchange for new cards?"

"One," he said, shoving a single discard through the counter well, the finality of the act smug, almost contemptuous.

Eugenia dealt him a card from the deck, then removed two cards from her own hand. Like Durham, she pushed the discards through the hole in the table, where they fell soundlessly to the drawer below. Her discard complete, she gave herself two new cards from the top of the deck.

She looked at her hand only once, not bothering to arrange the cards in any particular order, then laid them back down on the table.

"So, Papillion," Durham said, the words loud enough for all in the room to hear, "are you still residing here in Grosvenor Square with Seymour?"

Eugenia heard one gasp, then whispers beginning to

travel through the room. She knew why Durham had asked the question, to see if he could rattle her into doing something stupid. Without answering, she asked the dealer's required question: "Before we begin playing for tricks, does anyone wish to declare a flush?"

"As a matter of fact," Durham said, "I do."

With that, he laid down an ace-high flush in hearts. While he leaned back in his chair, a satisfied look on his face, a buzz of voices sounded all around them. "Well, *Mistress* Cardplayer," he said, "is play at an end?"

Quietly, Eugenia said, "I think not, my lord." Taking her time, she turned over her own cards, one at a time, until all five were visible.

"Clubs!" Mr. Martin Winfield shouted from somewhere behind her chair. "Capital. The lady has a flush in trumps!"

Eugenia honored her promise to Nathan, and amid shouts of congratulations and a smattering of applause, she gathered her ten thousand pounds and exited the drawing room. Knowing every eye was on her, she kept her head high while she climbed the stairs to the upper floor. Only when she was in her bedchamber, with the door locked, did she give way to the tremors that shook her body like an ague.

"I won it," she said, her voice so shaky it did not sound like her own. "I won the ten thousand!"

Excitement sustained her for as long as it took to disrobe and scrub her face clean of paint. Only after she had silently folded all the clothes she had gotten from Henrietta Parker, put them away in the chest of drawers, then placed the garnet necklace and earrings on top of the dressing table, did the excitement suddenly desert her. With its desertion, she was left with a feeling of deep despair, a despair that almost choked her.

She had completed the task for which she had begun

this foolish charade—to win back her cousin's lost inheritance—and now it was time to return to her own world, her own sphere. Time to leave Grosvenor Square. Time to leave Nathan Seymour, the man who would forever own her heart.

He might not want her heart or her love, but they were his nonetheless.

Knowing she would never sleep, Eugenia did not bother turning back the cover. Instead, she packed her trunk with those items she had brought with her, then donned the blue muslin dress she had worn the first day she came to this house. Lastly, she put the money she had won in her reticule and placed it and her brown faille pelisse at the foot of the bed. With nothing more to do, she sat down in the little blue-striped slipper chair to wait for dawn.

While she waited, she heard the guests down below in the street, their words of farewell drifting up through the window of her bedchamber. They were leaving in happy, boisterous groups, some in carriages, some on foot, at least one singing a rather bawdy ballad at the top of his lungs.

Finally, when all was quiet, she heard a soft knock at her door. "Eugenia," Nathan called, "are you still awake?"

She did not answer, and after a few moments, he said, "I know you are not asleep."

She remained silent.

"Please, Eugenia. Talk to me."

It took all her resolve to say nothing.

"I know you are angry with me," he said. "What I cannot determine is *why* you are angry. But I promise you this, no matter what the cause of the misunderstanding, we will straighten it out tomorrow. For now, all I wanted to tell you was that I am very proud of you."

A sob rose in Eugenia's throat. *No*, her soul cried, *do not tell me this. Not now.*

Nathan did not hear her silent plea. "You had a mission," he continued, "and you did not waver from it. Now you have accomplished your goal. You beat Lord Durham at his own game, and you did it with style." For a moment there was silence, then he said, "Brava, my brown-eyed Urania. Brava."

Eugenia heard nothing more through the thick door, and after a time, when she was certain that Nathan had gone to his own bedchamber, she felt the warm, salty tears spill down her cheeks. At first she brushed them away with the back of her hand, but when they continued to flow, she surrendered to the inevitable and let them be. They fell like rain, like a veritable flood of liquid sorrow.

Finally, spent both emotionally and physically, she cried herself to sleep, still sitting in the slipper chair. It was a deep sleep, partly because she had not slept the night before, and partly because of the heartbreak she had suffered for the past twenty-four hours.

Unfortunately, at that moment sleep was not her friend. It kept her from hearing the knife blade that was forced, oh so quietly, between the doorjamb and the lock. It kept her from hearing the door being opened. And it muffled the footfalls of the two men who crept into her room.

Chapter Sixteen

Eugenia thought she must be dreaming, for her body seemed to be floating on air. It was only when a man's hand clamped down across her mouth, squeezing cruelly, that she realized it was no dream; she was being lifted from the chair, held aloft by two men. Coming awake with frightening speed, she began to claw at the hand upon her mouth. Terrified, she twisted and turned, trying to break free of her captors.

"Damn 'er eyes!" said a rough voice. "She'll 'ave the 'ole 'ouse awake at this rate. Tie 'er feet quick like, Bertie, then see to 'er 'ands."

While his accomplice bound her ankles with a rope, Eugenia heard her captor say, "Don't know why we couldn't've just set the room afire like we did with that other whore. Much easier that way. But 'is nibs said 'e wanted this one brought to 'im. This time 'e wants 'is revenge personal like."

Quite certain she could guess the identity of the man who wanted to be revenged upon her, and terrified at the thought of being at his mercy, Eugenia tried once again to break free. She bit her captor's hand—bit it hard—but any triumph she may have felt at the deed was short lived. The man made her pay the price for her effrontery.

He spewed a string of profanity, crudities made all the more obscene because they were spoken directly into her ear. As he cursed, he forced a wadded rag between Eugenia's lips, all but ramming it down her throat; then he tied a cloth of some kind around her mouth to hold the gag in place. With a laugh, he gave the cloth a final, vicious twist that threatened to break her jaw. "See 'ow fast you bite a man after this."

While the accomplice finished binding her hands, her captor put a heavy sack over her head and forced her to her knees. "Find the money, Bertie, and be quick about it. 'Is nibs wants 'is gelt back, every last groat of it. And as mad as 'e is, I'd not want to be the one as told 'im we couldn't find it."

With her mouth bound and the sack over her head, Eugenia thought she must surely pass out from lack of air, but that was not to be the case. Without warning, the man dealt her a sharp blow to the back of her head, a blow that felt as though it had knocked her eyes right out of her skull. For an instant, the pain was intense; then, blessedly, she felt her body crumple to the floor, and she knew no more.

"Mr. Seymour!"

Dragged from a much-needed rest, Nathan heard the pounding; it sounded like a sledgehammer beating upon his bedchamber door.

"Sir!" called a rough, unfamiliar voice. "Wake up. It's me, Zeb Arnold. They've taken the lady."

Instantly awake, Nathan threw back the cover and ran to the door, yanking it open just before the ham-sized fist of the Bow Street runner pounded once again. The man held a single candlestick, but even in the dim light, Nathan could see the door to Eugenia's bedchamber. It had been forced open and now stood ajar.

Nathan pushed past the runner, compelled to see the room for himself. Aside from the door, nothing was disturbed. The bed was still neatly made, and across the counterpane lay Eugenia's brown pelisse, as if she meant to don the garment at any minute. As well, her trunk stood on the floor beside the bed table. The fact that the trunk was packed was not lost upon Nathan. Still, the room appeared to be in order. Nothing was missing. Nothing, that is, except the lady herself.

Striving to remain calm, Nathan returned to the corridor, where the runner waited. "Tell me what you know," he said.

"Not much, I'm sorry to say. The last I remember, the servants 'ad all gone to bed, and I was sittin' at the table in the kitchen, 'aving a wee bite. Just trying' one of them lobster patties, I was, when *whop*! some varlet cudgels me." He put his large hand to the back of his head. "I've a knot back 'ere the size of a goose egg, and me noggin feels like it's been used for a cricket ball. When I come to myself, the kitchen door stood open. No sign of anyone, though. Just the night mists drifting in."

The bisected eyebrow twitched. "Naturally, I ran up 'ere to check on the young lady." He cleared his throat. "I'm that sorry, Mr. Seymour, sir, for letting the varlet sneak up behind me. But we'll find the young lady, never you fear. Cooper will 'ave seen something. After the party, 'e slipped into the shadows across the street. Small like 'e is, 'e 'as a way of disappearing into the darkness. They'll not 'ave spied 'im there, I'll stake my life on it."

"Damn you!" Nathan said, frustration making him want to lash out at someone, "it is not *your* life at stake, is it?" He slammed his hand against the wall in mingled rage and anxiety. "I pray heaven it will not prove to be Eugenia's."

He turned then and hurried back to his dressing room, where he began yanking clothes from the chiffonnier. "If that swine has laid so much as a finger on her," he said, dragging a shirt over his head, "I vow I will do murder before this day is done."

Five minutes later, he was down in the kitchen, looking about for any sign of the intruders, searching for anything that might offer a clue to where they took Eugenia. Arnold showed him where he had been sitting when he was cudgeled, but aside from an overturned stool, there was no indication that anyone had been there.

"Sir?" said Riddle, who had come down in his dressing gown and slippers to see what the commotion was about, "can I be of any assistance?" Upon hearing of the abduction, the butler's face became a study in misery, and he began to pace back and forth, wringing his hands. "This is my fault. After that thief broke in, I should have had the locks changed."

He stopped his pacing long enough to look at his employer. "It was that blackguard, Weems, who took Miss Eugenia. I am certain of it. The fellow knew exactly which room she occupied, and he bore her a grudge. And he knew how to get into the house, having broken in once before."

Because the last sentence brought a mist to the servant's eyes, Nathan put his hand on the man's shoulder. "You are not to blame. Believe me, the fault is entirely mine. I knew what manner of man Durham was. I should have known he would do something like this."

Riddle blinked back the tears. "Lord Durham, sir? What has his lordship to do with Weems?"

"Durham employs the scoundrel. The runners have been following Weems for more than a week, and they have proof of the association."

As if suddenly struck with an idea, Nathan bid Riddle send someone to have the landau brought around. To the runner he said, "Go look for Cooper again. See if he has returned."

Arnold moved toward the door. "Yes, sir."

"If Cooper is back at his post, bring him to me. If he is

still missing, you and I will go alone. I think I know where we should start looking."

"Where did you have in mind, sir?"

"Pev'ny Lane," Nathan replied.

"The brothel. Of course. Should of thought of it myself, for 'tis a place where females are often took against their will. No one seeing it would remark a couple of louts carrying one more struggling body into the place."

Though it was no more than Nathan had reasoned for himself, hearing the words spoken in such a matter-of-fact manner nearly drove him mad. As he pictured Eugenia, bound and struggling, he took a step toward the runner, his hands balled into fists. "Damn you, Arnold, if you—"

"Mr. Seymour," said a cultured voice from just outside the kitchen door.

"Cooper!" Nathan said.

"Jack," said the runner.

If Riddle was surprised to see the short, balding gentleman who had been a guest at the card party, he kept the fact to himself. Too much was happening this evening for him to assimilate, and gentlemanly runners seemed to be all of a piece with everything else. Only later was he to discover that Gentleman Jack Cooper was one of Bow Street's most notable operatives.

"I followed them," Cooper said without preamble. "They took her to Pev'ny Lane. Lord Durham was waiting for them, I saw him in the light when the entrance door was opened. It being three against one, not to mention the pair of Neanderthals who guard the door, I thought it best to come back for Arnold before I tried to rescue the lady."

"We will all go," Nathan said.

While Riddle hurried around to the mews to have a team put to the landau, Nathan went to the library and removed a pocket pistol from the bottom drawer of the polished oak desk. After loading both barrels, he slipped the weapon inside his boot and hurried outside to the pavement to wait for the carriage.

Eugenia came awake slowly. Her head felt as if it had been used for a door knocker, and when she opened her eyes, the candlelight in the small, dank office stabbed her brain like a thousand shards of glass. Someone had yanked away the suffocating sack, leaving her hair falling all about her face, and they had also taken the gag out of her mouth. Unfortunately, her hands and feet were still bound, and the ropes were biting into the flesh at her wrists and ankles.

She lay in a corner, near a grime-encrusted window, and not five feet away, sitting behind an ugly, scarred desk was Cedric Durham. His lordship was counting a small stack of money. "It is all here," he said, putting the pound notes in a metal box on the desk, then tossing what looked like Eugenia's reticule onto the floor.

" 'Course it's all there, my lord. You know you can trust me."

Jem Weems! Eugenia had thought she recognized the voice when she was being abducted.

Durham looked at the man in the laborer's smock. "Yes, I trust you," he said, his tone conversational, almost as if he were discussing the weather. "I trust you because you know I would kill you if you should prove unreliable."

The words sent a cold chill through Eugenia, a chill that turned icy when Durham reached inside the top drawer of the desk and pulled out a holster pistol. It was a long-barrel pistol, the kind men often carried on their saddles. He aimed the weapon directly at Jem Weems's head, and both Weems and his cohort took a step back. From the frightened looks on their faces, they did not take Durham's threat lightly; they did not, and neither did Eugenia.

Cedric Durham was a known bully, and he had obviously sent Fiona's "uncle" and the sweep to Grosvenor Square to abduct the woman who had made him lose face at the loo table. Would he take the final step, she wondered, from abductor to murderer?

"Get out of here," Durham said to the men, "before I blast holes through your worthless hides."

The sweep made a hasty retreat, but Weems stood his ground. "What about me money?" he said. "I brought that tart to you like you said, and the ten thousand quid as well. Me and Bertie deserve sommit for our troubles. The way I figure it, you owe us for—"

"You stupid lout! How dare you tell me what I owe you!"

Durham crashed his chair against the wall, then walked around to the side of the desk. "The way *I* figure it," he said, mimicking the other man's broad cockney, "you still owe *me* for the little guttersnipe who escaped through the window. Who can say how much that cost me, for I had half a dozen gentlemen willing to bid against each other for the right to be first to bed the girl."

Eugenia very nearly threw up. He was talking about Fiona, the spunky little maid Nathan had saved, a little girl who could never seem to get enough food to compensate for a childhood too often spent hungry.

"See 'ere now," Weems said, "I brought 'er 'ere all right and tight. It was them two lummoxes as is supposed to guard the place, they let 'er get away." He looked as if he meant to continue to argue his case, but all he got for his trouble was a knock in the forehead with the metal-covered grip of Durham's pistol.

Immediately, blood began to spurt from the wound and ran down the man's startled face. He fell back against the wall, where he struggled to maintain his balance. After several seconds, however, his knees seemed to give way, and he slid slowly to the floor.

If Eugenia had ever believed the maxim about honor among thieves, she believed it no longer. At the first sign of trouble, Bertie, the chimney sweep, had fled the room, abandoning his friend in hopes of saving his own skin. As for Lord Durham, he was a man totally without honor. He was a bully, a cheat, and a seller of innocent children, and judging from the blood pouring from the fallen man's forehead, his lordship was soon to be a murderer.

Showing no more emotion than if he had merely squashed a bug, Durham shoved the pistol into his waistcoat, then bent and reached his hand inside Weems's smock. When he stood again, he held the knife Weems had brandished the day he and the chimney sweep came to the town house in pursuit of Fiona.

When Durham turned toward Eugenia, she thought her heart would stop, for he held the knife as if intending to use it. She said a quick prayer and squeezed her eyes shut, not wanting Durham's face to be the last she saw upon this earth, but to her relief, he did not slit her throat. Instead, he bent down and sawed through the ropes tied around her ankles.

After tossing the knife aside, he grabbed Eugenia by the bodice of her dress and pulled her to her feet. "And now, Papillion, you and I are going up to one of the rooms, where I will show you the price you must pay for having made a fool of Cedric Durham."

When Eugenia tried to pull away from him, he gave her a shake that threatened to loosen her teeth. "Do not anger me further," he warned, retrieving the pistol and jabbing the end of the cold, unyielding barrel into the hollow of her throat.

"No, no," she said, stalling for time, hoping some plan

of escape might present itself before the villain got her abovestairs, "I will be good."

"Actually," he said, "you would be wise to employ your many skills to please me as you obviously pleased Nathan Seymour, for once I grow tired of you, I mean to send you to one of my other brothels."

Nathan had the coachman stop the landau some little distance from Pev'ny Lane. He and Gentleman Jack Cooper, a man whose keen insight into the criminal mind made him far more dangerous than the powerfully built Zeb Arnold, had agreed upon a plan. Nathan and Arnold would seek admittance through the front door of the shabby-looking brick residence, pretending to be customers, and if necessary, they would immobilize the pair of Neanderthals who guarded the entrance.

In the meantime, the much smaller Cooper would climb through the window that looked onto the alley. In that way, they might have the added advantage of attack from two sides.

"Open up," Nathan called, slurring his words as if inebriated. He pounded on the heavy front door. "Open up, I say. We've come for a little fun."

One of the guards opened the door halfway, the single candle in his hand offering little illumination in the darkened vestibule. He was a big man, though not so fit as Zeb Arnold, and he used his bulk to block their path. "You're too late," he said, yawning wide to reveal decaying molars. "We're closed. Come back tomorrow."

"Aw, come on," Nathan pleaded, "Ish not all that late. The sun's not up yet. Let us in, there's a good chap." He reached into his pocket and produced a golden sovereign. "This ish for you," he said, purposely dropping the coin onto the carpet so the man would be obliged to step aside to retrieve it.

While the guard bent to get the gold coin, Nathan

squeezed through the space between the man and the door. "Rumor has it you've got somebody new in there," he said. "Heard somebody say they saw her being brought in. All tied up like a Christmas present, she was. Let us have a look at her. What d'ya say?"

"You've been lied to," the man said, his voice surly. "There ain't nobody new. Now get back outside, or I'll throw you out myself."

"Here, now," said a voice from somewhere inside the house, "wot's all this racket?"

The second guard came toward them. He carried a branch of candles, and in the greater light, Nathan spied something shiny on the garish red carpet. It was a little silver swan, the swan Eugenia had worn in her hair that evening.

At sight of the silver pin lying there forlorn and totally out of place, Nathan went a bit crazy. Acting more like an enraged animal than a civilized gentleman, he bent forward and charged the approaching guard, landing his shoulder in the man's solar plexus and felling him with the unexpected attack.

Zeb Arnold, not waiting for an invitation to join the fracas, threw his massive body against the door, hitting it with such force it banged against the wall, dislodging a cheap, gold-leaf girandole looking glass that shattered into a million pieces. "Seven years bad luck," the runner said. "For you!"

The guard, his mouth agape with surprise, watched as Zeb Arnold's sledgehammer fist sped toward his face. It connected with his jaw, and down the man went with the reverberating noise of a falling tree.

Nathan rescued the candelabrum before it set the rug afire, and as he held the light aloft, a wizened little man—a chimney sweep if ground-in smut was anything to go by—came running from the back of the house. The fellow paused when he saw the commotion in the vestibule, and for a moment he looked as if he could not decide whether to go forward or return the way he came.

"Stay where you are!" Nathan demanded.

He passed the candelabrum to Zeb Arnold, then removed the pocket pistol from his boot. He aimed the weapon at the little man's chest. "We are looking for a young woman," he said, "and those two sorry specimens on the floor denied any knowledge of her, sorely taxing my good nature. Therefore, if you are wise, you will tell me what I want to know before my patience is totally exhausted. Where is the lady you abducted?"

"I have her," said a voice Nathan recognized immediately. "Were you wishful of speaking with her, Seymour?"

Nathan's breath all but deserted him when he spied Durham coming from the rear of the house. The coward had his arm around Eugenia's waist, holding her in front of him like a shield, and the barrel of his pistol was boring into the side of her neck.

Her brown eyes were wide with fear, and at the sight of her at Durham's mercy, Nathan felt as though an iron fist had dealt him a blow to the heart. "Damn you, Durham! If you have hurt her, I swear I will kill you with my bare hands."

"*Tsk tsk*, Seymour. Such passion. Could it be that this little tart means more to you than any of your usual mistresses? Never knew you to take such an interest in any one female." He laughed, though the sound had little humor in it. "Most imprudent of you, don't you know, for it renders you quite vulnerable."

He pushed the barrel harder into Eugenia's neck, making her wince with the pain. "Now drop your pistol, or I will let you watch me put a hole right through this pretty white throat."

Nathan moved as if to surrender his weapon, but Eugenia cried out. "Do not, Nathan! Lord Durham is deranged, and once you are disarmed, he will not hesitate to kill you."

"I must," Nathan said. "I cannot let him hurt you."

"Please," she said. "You cannot trust him. He has already committed one murder this night. I could not bear it if he killed you."

"How very touching," Durham said. "Two lovebirds, each willing to be sacrificed for the other. Perhaps I should shoot you both and let you finish this little scene in eternity."

"No!" Nathan shouted, "do not hurt her."

"Then do as I say, or I—Aaagh!"

For a moment, no one moved; it was as if they were all part of a tableau enacted for the amusement of some unseen audience. Then Lord Durham's arm fell away from Eugenia's waist, and the hand holding the pistol to her neck went limp.

Nathan reached out and grabbed Eugenia by her bound wrists. He snatched her away from Durham, and without her support the man pitched forward, falling facedown on the floor. It was only after he fell that Nathan saw the crudely crafted knife protruding from Durham's back.

Not two feet away, a man with blood all over his face and smock stared down at the lifeless body. He swayed, as if he had expended the last of his life force. " 'E killed me," the man said, the words little more than a death rattle, "and now I've killed 'im back."

"Weems," Eugenia muttered, as the man collapsed beside Lord Durham's body.

" 'Tis a sorry end when thieves fall out," said a voice coming from the direction of the room where Eugenia had lain on the floor only moments ago. "When they perish together, there are none left to mourn their passing."

Eugenia gasped, for the speaker was the short, balding gentleman who had given her the five hundred pounds at the loo table. Now, instead of cards, he held a pistol in his hand. "It would appear," he said, "that I took too long getting through that window." He made Eugenia a gallant bow. "Forgive me, ma'am, I am not usually so tardy."

Chapter Seventeen

"But I still do not understand about Mr. Cooper," Eugenia said.

"Gentleman Jack, you mean."

While the landau rolled over the cobblestone street on its way to Grosvenor Square, Nathan used his fingers to comb Eugenia's hair back from her face; then he secured the silver swan among the dark brown tresses. She did not chastise him for the familiarity, perhaps because she was already sitting flush against his side, with his arm draped protectively across her shoulders.

Each time he looked at her wrists and saw the rope burns, Nathan was reminded of the moment he saw Durham using Eugenia as a human shield, his pistol aimed at her neck. Never in his life had Nathan known such gut-wrenching fear. Until that moment, he had not known that such fear existed. When he thought of what could so easily have happened to her at the hands of that maniac, he felt sick. He wanted to take her in his arms and never let her go.

"Gentleman Jack?" she said, bringing his thoughts back to her question.

"He is a distant cousin of Winny's. It was to him Winny and I went the day we returned from Hertfordshire. I do not know who actually employs the fellow, the Home Office or Bow Street, but he is a very handy man

to have around. After he heard the entire story about
Durham's ownership of that infamous brothel, Cooper
was happy to give us whatever help we needed. He knew
we could not just accuse a peer of such a crime; first, ir-
refutable evidence had to be gathered."

"Is that what he was doing sitting at Durham's table,
playing loo? Was he gathering evidence?"

"No. He was there to protect you. I already knew that
Durham was a bully. Until this past week, however, I did
not know his character was totally depraved. I could not
let you play cards with such a man without someone
nearby should you need assistance."

"No wonder you wanted to cancel the card party. I
wish you had told me your reasons, instead of offering to
give me the ten thousand." She tilted her head, trying to
see his face in the gray dawn light. "I . . . I totally misunderstood."

"Did you?" he said, captivated by her upturned face,
and fighting a strong desire to kiss her soft lips.

"Yes," she said. "I thought you offered me the money
so I would . . . uh . . ." She paused, obviously embarrassed, but she took a steadying breath and continued. "I
thought you wanted me to become your mistress."

"My what!"

Eugenia had been embarrassed enough telling him
what she thought; with his incredulity at the idea, she
positively burned with mortification.

If he felt a similar embarrassment, however, he hid the
fact quite well. In fact, Eugenia thought she detected a
slight pull at the corner of his mouth, as if he might be
smiling, but she told herself it was a trick of the still pale
light.

"So," he said, "you thought I wanted another mistress.
What if I had asked you to come live with me? To let me
love you? To let me show you the joys of passion that

only a man and woman can know? What would you have said?"

Eugenia looked away, avoiding his gaze, afraid she might betray how much she wanted to experience those joys with Nathan. It would be so easy to say yes. She loved him so much. Tonight she had been nearly paralyzed with fear, thinking that Lord Durham might shoot him. At that moment, Eugenia would have sold her immortal soul to save the life of the man she loved.

Would it be so very wrong to let him love her, regardless of the consequences? It would be wonderful to be with him; her heart told her that much. Paradise to lie in his arms. Bliss to wake up beside him. Sheer delight to know that he was there each morning and would be there again that night, wanting only her. It would be heaven, at least for a time.

But what about later, when he grew restless for a new love? How would Eugenia find the courage to go on without him?

"You are very quiet, Eugenia. Have you no answer to my question? Will you let me love you?"

Unable to say the words that would break her heart, she shook her head.

"No?" he asked.

"No."

"Not even if I tell you that I love you more than life itself? Even if I tell you that my life would be unbearably empty without you in it every day? Empty without your voice. Your touch. Your smile?"

Eugenia was not certain how much more of this she could endure without bursting into tears.

"Eugenia," he said softly, the one word sounding like a caress. "Eugenia, my love. Look at me, please."

She could not resist the gentle plea, and when she lifted her gaze, what she saw made her heart pound

painfully. From within his gray eyes shone a look of such
gentleness, such passion, that it could only be love.

"You came to me, my sweet Eugenia, because you
needed a scoundrel to help you catch a scoundrel." He
cradled her cheek in his palm, while his thumb moved
slowly, mesmerizingly across her lips. "Here is a
scoundrel who is yours for the taking. Take any or all of
me. My heart, my home, my name. Only say that you will
marry me and let me spend the rest of my life with you."

Eugenia could not believe the joy that filled her. "You
want to marry me?"

"Yes, my sweet. With all my heart."

He pulled her to him then and lowered his mouth to
hers, kissing her with a tenderness that promised ecstasy
to come. When the kiss deepened, her senses came alive,
and she was happier than she could ever remember being.

After a time, when he lifted his head, she snuggled
against his chest, content to be close to him, even if it was
in a carriage traveling over bumpy cobblestones.

"If you have no objections," he said, "I should like to
be married in the church at Stanton-on-Lee."

"Um," she said, "that sounds perfect."

"As well, because we have already flaunted the con-
ventions, I believe it would be best if we posted the
banns. No special license for us. We will offer no more
grist for the gossip mills. Until time for the ceremony, I
think I should return you to your aunt."

Eugenia sat up straight. "No. Not her."

Reminded of Lady Bailey, Eugenia recalled the ten
thousand pounds she had won from Durham. Somehow,
it no longer mattered that her aunt know she had reclaimed the money; Eugenia knew, and that was enough.
Tonight she had witnessed what the desire for revenge
could do to a person, and she wanted nothing more to do
with that insidious emotion. She would send the money

by special messenger to her cousin, and that would be the end to it.

"No," she repeated, "I will not go to my aunt."

"Then you must go back to the school and the Misses Beechbark."

"Becknell," Eugenia said. "But why must I go anywhere? Can I not remain at the town house?"

"No, my love. For one thing, you are far too tempting a morsel, and I fear if you are close by, I will not be able to resist sampling your sweetness."

Eugenia smiled, finding nothing to dislike in this possibility.

"For another thing," he continued, "by afternoon, the news of Durham's death will be all over town, and every busybody in Mayfair will be trying to discover all the sordid particulars. I want you well out of the way before that happens.

"Besides," he added, "I have some business to transact with Gentleman Jack Cooper, business that may take the better part of a week."

Eugenia knew a moment of apprehension. "Is there something you have not told me? You will not have to appear before a magistrate?"

He shook his head. "Bow Street will take care of all that. Since Durham and Weems killed each other, that should put an end to the investigation. However, those two were not the only victims in that dreadful place."

"The children," Eugenia said, suddenly ashamed that she had been so caught up in her own life she had forgotten about those unfortunate youngsters. "What will become of them?"

"I do not know. Cooper believes some of them may have been stolen from parents and homes. If that is the case, and they wish it, I propose to see them returned safely to their families. For those who have no homes, Cooper knows a school where the girls can be taught domestic skills so they can go into service. I have vouched for all fees and expenses."

"Oh, Nathan. You are surely the kindest man I have ever known, for you—"

He touched his finger to her lips to silence her. "I am nothing of the kind, my sweet. I may not be the scoundrel you once thought me, but I am far from a paragon."

She kissed his finger, then removed it from her lips. "A paragon? No, you are far from perfect. You are just a man who has learned all the essential lessons."

"Ah, yes, your mother's teachings. I am sorry to disappoint you, my love, but I cannot even recall the list."

"You do not need to remember them, for you live them. You are true to yourself. You are always fair. And you treat others as you would wish to be treated by them. Lastly," she said, "you have done more than one deed that will leave this earth a little better for your having lived upon it."

When he would have protested, she said, "You helped Fiona escape from a life of degradation, and you mean to aid the children from that awful place. And, of course, you saved me. Though whether that qualifies as making the world a better place, I cannot say. It—"

He silenced her with a kiss that made her forget there was anyone or anything in the universe but Nathan and the joy of his arms around her. "My wonderful girl," he muttered against her lips, "surely you know that you *are* my world."

As if to assure himself that she understood him, he took her face between his hands, gently, tenderly, then looked deeply into her eyes. "Madam instructress," he said, his voice slightly husky, "you bade me teach you how to catch a scoundrel. However, the final, the most important lesson of all was the one *you* taught me, for it was the lesson of love."

Epilogue

The London Times, *August 27, 1814*

Lately, Mr. Nathan Seymour of Swanleigh Hall, Hertfordshire, and Miss Eugenia Bailey, of Haselmere, Surrey. The bride wore a dress of white Spitalfields silk, whose only adornment was a single silver pin fashioned in the shape of a swan.

The groom was attended by a friend of long standing, Mr. Martin Winfield. The bride, a teacher in a female academy, was attended by her former employers, the Misses Agnes and Edwina Bakewell.

TALES OF LOVE AND ADVENTURE

☐**SHADES OF THE PAST by Sandra Heath.** A plunge through a trapdoor in time catapulted Laura Reynolds from the modern London stage into the scandalous world of Regency England, where a woman of the theater was little better than a girl of the streets. And it was here that Laura was cast in a drama of revenge against wealthy, handsome Lord Blair Deveril. (187520—$4.99)

☐**THE CAPTAIN'S DILEMMA by Gail Eastwood.** Perhaps if bold and beautiful Merissa Pritchard had not grown so tired of country life and her blue-blooded suitor, it would not have happened. Whatever the reason, Merissa had given the fleeing French prisoner of war, Captain Alexandre Valmont, a hiding place on her family estate. Even more shocking, she had given him entry into her heart. (181921—$4.50)

☐**THE IRISH RAKE by Emma Lange.** Miss Gillian Edwards was barely more than a schoolgirl—and certainly as innocent as one—but she knew how shockingly evil the Marquess of Clare was. He did not even try to hide a history of illicit loves that ran the gamut from London lightskirts to highborn ladies. Nor did he conceal his scorn for marriage and morality and his devotion to the pleasures of the flesh. (187687—$4.99)

Prices slightly higher in Canada

Payable in U.S. funds only. No cash/COD accepted. Postage & handling: U.S./CAN. $2.75 for one book, $1.00 for each additional, not to exceed $6.75; Int'l $5.00 for one book, $1.00 each additional. We accept Visa, Amex, MC ($10.00 min.), checks ($15.00 fee for returned checks) and money orders. Call 800-788-6262 or 201-933-9292, fax 201-896-8569; refer to ad #SRR1

Penguin Putnam Inc.
P.O. Box 12289, Dept. B
Newark, NJ 07101-5289
Please allow 4-6 weeks for delivery.
Foreign and Canadian delivery 6-8 weeks.

Bill my: ☐Visa ☐MasterCard ☐Amex_____(expires)
Card#_____
Signature_____

Bill to:
Name_____
Address_____ City_____
State/ZIP_____
Daytime Phone #_____

Ship to:
Name_____ Book Total $_____
Address_____ Applicable Sales Tax $_____
City_____ Postage & Handling $_____
State/ZIP_____ Total Amount Due $_____

This offer subject to change without notice.

DILEMMAS OF THE HEART

☐ **THE SILENT SUITOR by Elisabeth Fairchild.** Miss Sarah Wilkes Lyndle was stunningly lovely. Nonetheless, she was startled to have two of the leading lords drawn to her on her very first visit to London. One was handsome, elegant, utterly charming Stewart Castleford, known in society as "Beauty," and the other was his cousin Lord Ashley Hawkes Castleford, nicknamed "Beast." Sarah found herself on the horns of a dilemma.   (180704—$3.99)

☐ **THE AWAKENING HEART by Dorothy Mack.** The lovely Dinah Elcott finds herself in quite a predicament when she agrees to pose as a marriageable miss in public to the elegant Charles Talbot. In return, he will let Dinah pursue her artistic ambitions in private, but can she resist her own untested and shockingly susceptible heart?   (178254—$3.99)

☐ **LORD ASHFORD'S WAGER by Marjorie Farrell.** Lady Joanna Barrand knows all there is to know about Lord Tony Ashford—his gambling habits, his wooing of a beautiful older widow to rescue him from ruin and, worst of all, his guilt in a crime that makes all his other sins seem innocent. What she doesn't know is how she has lost her heart to him.   (180496—$3.99)

Prices slightly higher in Canada

Payable in U.S. funds only. No cash/COD accepted. Postage & handling: U.S./CAN. $2.75 for one book, $1.00 for each additional, not to exceed $6.75; Int'l $5.00 for one book, $1.00 each additional. We accept Visa, Amex, MC ($10.00 min.), checks ($15.00 fee for returned checks) and money orders. Call 800-788-6262 or 201-933-9292, fax 201-896-8569; refer to ad # SRR2

Penguin Putnam Inc.   Bill my: ☐Visa ☐MasterCard ☐Amex_____(expires)
P.O. Box 12289, Dept. B   Card#_____
Newark, NJ 07101-5289   Signature_____
Please allow 4-6 weeks for delivery.
Foreign and Canadian delivery 6-8 weeks.

Bill to:
Name_____
Address_____City_____
State/ZIP_____
Daytime Phone #_____

Ship to:
Name_____ Book Total $_____
Address_____ Applicable Sales Tax $_____
City_____ Postage & Handling $_____
State/ZIP_____ Total Amount Due $_____

This offer subject to change without notice.

ROMANCE FROM THE PAST

☐ **THE WICKED GROOM by April Kihlstrom.** It was bad enough when Lady Diana Westcott learned her parents were wedding her to the infamous Duke of Berenford. But it was even worse when she came face-to-face with him. First he disguised his identity to gain a most improper access to her person. Then he hid the beautiful woman in his life even as that passion of the past staked a new claim to his ardent affection. Now Diana had to deceive this devilish deceiver about how strongly she responded to his kisses and how weak she felt in his arms.   (187504—$4.99)

☐ **THE SECRET NABOB by Martha Kirkland.** Miss Madeline Wycliff's two sisters were as different as night and day. One was bold and brazen and had wed a rake whose debts now threatened the family estate; but the other was as untouched as she was exquisite. Now Madeline had to turn her back on love and get dangerously close to a nefarious nabob to save her sister's happiness and innocence...even if it meant sacrificing her own.   (187377—$4.50)

☐ **A HEART POSSESSED by Katherine Sutcliffe.** From the moment Ariel Rushdon was reunited with Lord Nicholas Wyndham, the lover who had abandoned her, she could see the torment in his eyes. Now she would learn the secrets of his house. Now she would learn the truth about his wife's death. And now she would also make Nick remember everything—their wild passion, their sacred vows...their child....
                                                                          (407059—$5.50)

Prices slightly higher in Canada

Payable in U.S. funds only. No cash/COD accepted. Postage & handling: U.S./CAN. $2.75 for one book, $1.00 for each additional, not to exceed $6.75; Int'l $5.00 for one book, $1.00 each additional. We accept Visa, Amex, MC ($10.00 min.), checks ($15.00 fee for returned checks) and money orders. Call 800-788-6262 or 201-933-9292, fax 201-896-8569; refer to ad #SRR4

Penguin Putnam Inc.   Bill my: ☐ Visa ☐ MasterCard ☐ Amex _____ (expires)
P.O. Box 12289, Dept. B   Card#_____
Newark, NJ 07101-5289   Signature_____
Please allow 4-6 weeks for delivery.
Foreign and Canadian delivery 6-8 weeks.

Bill to:
Name_____
Address_____City_____
State/ZIP_____
Daytime Phone #_____

Ship to:
Name_____   Book Total $_____
Address_____   Applicable Sales Tax $_____
City_____   Postage & Handling $_____
State/ZIP_____   Total Amount Due $_____
                    This offer subject to change without notice.